BEWITCHED VIKING

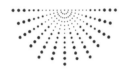

REE THORNTON

COPYRIGHT

Cover by Exposed Publishing: https://www.facebook.com/ XposedBookDesign

ACKNOWLEDGMENTS

Thank you to Dana Mitchell, Sara Hartland, L.J. Langdon, Elsa Holland, Josie Baker, and Tanya Nellestein for the fabulous feedback and encouragement. And a special shout out to Jo from Exposed Publishing for your endless patience in creating another fabulous cover.

DEDICATION

For my littlest sister, Eva, who leaves behind footsteps sprinkled with magic. Loving you made me a better person. I am so proud of you.

CHAPTER ONE

IVVÀR

*S*houlders stiff and hands clasped behind his back, Ivvár Eriksson stood awaiting the judgment of the assembly of the *Thing*. King Ake Sorensen sat in his high-backed wooden chair atop the snow-covered knoll, the rest of the assembly forming a semi-circle of nation elders around him.

Behind them, a gold chain hung from the gables of the Uppsala temple, glistening in the late-winter sun, a shiny beacon calling forth those destined for the sacrifice of the dísablót. Beyond the temple, bodies swung from branches in the sacred grove, their blood reddening the earth as it had the stone shrine in offering to honor the dísarsalr, the hall of the goddess.

Every nine years, the vernal equinox brought nine days of bloodshed for a plentiful harvest. All gathered in the sacred grove at twilight to honor the nine heads of every living thing offered in the *blót*. Blood fell to the earth, accompanied by the rhythmic drumming and the haunting ritual songs of the priestesses, and the veil between the gods and men lifted.

As gnarled branches of sacred trees groaned under the weight of the offerings hoisted aloft, the air crackled with rising anticipation. Pleasing the gods would chase away the strong shadows of winter.

Would that be *his* destiny? For his blood to be cast to the earth as an offering to the Dísir, the bloodthirsty female spirits of his ancestors? Or would he be outlawed for his misdeed? Although a minor infraction against a king, it was so foolish, he realized now in hindsight.

Verdicts in a *Thing* were unpredictable. The machinations of those who wielded power, the tug of war of alliances, old vengeances souring under the surface, and leverageable debts. His father had ensured the Erikssons were powerful, a clan not to be crossed. And tales of his and his brothers' prowess with the sword had long been fodder for the songs of the traveling scalds. Yet he was unsure that either his family's power or popularity would save him this day.

"Ivvár Eriksson..."

Ivvár swung his wary gaze back to the man he had wronged—King Ake Sorensen.

The king narrowed his gaze, worry lines forming around his eyes that matched his greying hair and beard. Though his warrior days were behind him, and his weathered face betrayed his advancing years, there was no mistaking the man's power—King Ake controlled the assembly with a combination of fear and begrudging respect for his shrewd mind.

Ivvár straightened his back and prepared for the worst. Being a sacrifice to the Dísir would still restore his honor, and that was important. He would not cower or shame his kin.

The lawspeaker, a small man with a stoic countenance

and uncommonly soft hands, entered the sacred circle of the *Thing* and motioned Ivvár forward.

Holding his head high, Ivvár approached the assembly.

"Ivvár Eriksson, you are accused of theft." The lawspeaker's gaze became distant, his voice a soft languid drawl as he recited the law. "Theft. The sentence for such crime may be payment of reparations as demanded by those you have wronged, outlawry, or the exchange of blood to honor the gods. What say you to this charge?"

"I am guilty of the crime charged and shall face my fate with honor."

The lawspeaker nodded at him respectfully. "Ivvár Eriksson is hereby found guilty of theft. The assembly will deliver the sentence."

Ivvár turned to face the assembly and the man who would decide his fate. Committing a crime against a victim who could not or was not present to defend themselves was considered the worst of all, but he had reclaimed some honor in admitting to the wrong.

King Ake began to speak, not even bothering to feign any illusion of consultation with those seated around him. This verdict would be his and his alone. "Ivvár Eriksson, for the crime of theft, you are sentenced to marry."

Ivvár gasped, his mouth suddenly parched. "Wed?" His voice fractured into a throaty croak as he forced the word out.

A twitter of laughter spread through the crowd. People traveled to Uppsala to bear witness to the Dísir sacrifices. Along with the solemn purpose of their gathering, was the pleasure of many distant villages coming together and plying their wares at the *dísting* market. But of all the events, the favored pastime was observing law disputes at the *Thing* and discovering the shameful secrets the accused had failed to keep hidden. His verdict had just made him the top of the list for their amusement.

Ivvár cast a scathing look at the loudest group of onlookers. Three moons had passed since that foolish, drunken moment, yet a much-embellished version of the tale was still shared around campfires.

Word that one of the renowned Eriksson brothers was to be sentenced had spread like wildfire through the encampment. And now they would whisper and jest of the ironic justice of a notorious skirt-chaser being forced to wed.

All for a deer. A drunken wager and a deer.

Ivvár shook his head in disgust as their whispers continued unabated. He had fought alongside many of these warriors. They would undoubtedly celebrate the downfall of their greatest rival for women's affections. Would the womenfolk lament the loss of an accomplished bedmate?

"Wed?" he repeated, still in shock. He'd expected a harsh sentence for poaching on the King's land, and his honor forced him to admit that he deserved to be punished for the foolhardy wager taken in a moment of weakness, but not this.

Not marriage.

Marriage on command made him look like a fool, would make a mockery of him every time anyone saw him with his wife and children for the rest of his life.

"I am a warrior," he said, his tone steadfast.

Quirking a bushy eyebrow, King Ake leaned back and crossed his arms over his chest. "Hunting on my lands without leave." The king's green eyes moved up and down over his person as though scanning for the worth of the man before him and finding him lacking.

Ivvár clenched his hands tight, nails digging into his palms. He was a warrior of honor, not a thief, as the king well knew. King Ake had refused his offer of gold coins for the deer, choosing instead to call him before the *Thing*. To punish him, humiliate him.

The King's greying beard swayed back and forth as he shook his head in disapproval. "It is no small affront, yet I am loath to declare 'outlaw' the son of my friend Ràsmus Eriksson. Let a wife temper your rebellious urges, Ivvár. And keep you far from my lands and my deer."

"Forcing a marriage is not a punishment."

"It is for one such as you."

Ivvár glanced at each of the three women and nine men chosen to pass judgment on those disputes brought to the *Thing* assembly. Each sat on a high-backed oak chair carved with renderings of the gods, their wrinkled faces and vacant stares as intimidating as the chilling silence surrounding them.

His heart sank, all hope of another resolution vanishing like the sun at midwinter. *He would find no honor here.* All knew that King Ake controlled the outcome this day.

Ivvár glanced over his shoulder at his twin brother, Rorik.

Legs spread and arms folded, his twin stood just beyond the ropes strung between the hazelnut poles that marked the sacred, hallowed ground of the *Thing*.

Before their eyes even met, Ivvàr knew that Rorik's were lit with fury. He could feel his twin's anger scorching him from the inside through their twin bond.

Ivvár turned back to face the king with renewed determination. He had no desire to take a wife and put down roots— likely he never would. There were too many ports to visit, ales to drink, and women to bed. His lips opened, his mind forming the last-chance words needed to secure his freedom from such an unfortunate fate.

King Ake's lips pressed into a hard line, and his right eyebrow arched.

Ivvár could almost hear the unspoken words behind the man's simple gesture. *You dare question me, boy?*

His chest tightened, apprehension rising like a cresting wave that broke and washed away all his confidence. Who was he to think he could make a king bend to his will? He might be able to talk his way into any woman's furs, but King Ake was no woman. Besides, not all marriages lasted—they could be dissolved.

The King's brow furrowed at being made to wait, but he said naught.

Ivvár slammed his mouth shut. Questioning the king's judgment inside the sacred circle of the *Thing* would be a grave insult, worse even than his crime of poaching.

Ivvàr lowered his gaze, showing deference although he could not bring himself to voice acquiescence. Marriages were negotiated to form alliances and bond families to each other, not to be handed out as punishment for crimes. What woman would accept a bond arising from such ill beginnings? Mayhap, there lay a chance for this farce to end.

"You came to be judged. You have not shamed the Eriksson name," King Ake said with begrudging respect.

Ivvár remained silent. His gaze rose, and out of habit, his fingers sought and tightened around the hilt of his sword. The cool familiar steel against his palm soothed his frayed nerves. Should he make another proposal of recompense? Mayhap, he could offer the king the use of his sword and make use of the battle prowess of which the Eriksson brothers were renowned.

King Ake's jaw tensed, his eyes blazing with a dangerous calm.

Ivvár's heart raced as he weighed his options. Everything

he had heard about this man was the truth. Ake Sorensen had held his throne since boyhood, a feat achieved by drenching the earth with the blood of his enemies until none dared challenge the Viking king who had led his men into battle astride a black stallion. He was a formidable enemy with a long memory.

Ivvár relaxed his grip on his weapon and let his hand fall to his side. No coin or promises would right this wrong, and he suspected that the mere suggestion would result in swift and painful punishment. He gave a slight nod of surrender, his stomach roiling as last eve's ale threatened to come back up.

The tension eased from King Ake's shoulders before he turned and motioned someone forward from the crowd that watched beyond the ropes.

Unease crept up his spine. *What was the old man doing now?*

A sudden gust of wind whirled across the snow-covered knoll. Faces turned away, unbound hair whipping wildly as those with coats pulled them tighter and held fast.

Ivvár looked to the skies, scanning for gathering storm clouds as the sense of foreboding rose. Not a cloud could be seen, yet the sudden wind suggested the gods were at play with the fates of men. The gust eased as swiftly as it had begun, and his gaze returned to the assembly before him.

A figure hidden beneath a hooded cape stepped over the rope enclosing the sacred ground and glided to a stop beside King Ake.

Ivvàr studied the slender figure that stood barely higher than the king's high-backed chair, curious at the untimely intrusion. The cape was unusual—a deep blue color rarely used on such large garments given the expense of the indigo powder that could only be found in the lands far to the east.

Held together by a gold pin brooch at the chest, the cape opened as it fell around the hem of a red dress and brown leather boots.

A woman's small hand extended from the thick fabric and settled on the back of King Ake's chair, her other hand holding a staff carved of the sacred ash tree with an ornate steel cap at the top and tassels of beads and feathers.

Völva!

The cape wearer was a priestess. He'd not heard of King Ake having a völva, yet it made sense that one of the priest-esses coveted for their mastery of magic and healing would aid him.

Delicate fingers lifted to push back the hood that shrouded the woman's face in shadow. The crown of her head was bathed in bright beams of sunlight that sent a shimmer across hair the same shade as a sunset.

The völva kept her gaze lowered, her dark auburn hair rippling across her face as she looked down at the giant cat with thick orange and white mottled fur curling and twisting around her slender ankles.

Purring contentedly, the cat nimbly stepped over her feet.

An unfamiliar yearning to see her face struck. *Who was she? Was a forced marriage not punishment enough? Had the king called on her to curse him?* That would be a cruel fate indeed—to be allowed to live yet cursed forevermore.

Ivvár studied this new threat, his gaze skimming down over the flame-colored locks that blended with the vibrant raspberry hue of her fine-quality dress. His pulse quickened at the magic surrounding her. He could feel it pulling at him, seducing him with a tantalizing promise of danger. His cock stirred. Was this what he'd heard men speak of? The lustful erotic lures the völva used to entice warriors to their deaths.

He leaned forward, curious to see more.

King Ake spoke to her in a hushed whisper and then looked back at him.

What was the man plotting?

The priestess turned to face the crowd, her chin slowly lifting into the poised, proud bearing of one assured of their power.

Ivvàr stumbled back a step, shaken.

A layer of white clay covered her oval face like freshly fallen snow on a midwinter morning, a stark contrast to the three thick black lines that slashed from her forehead to her eyebrow and then again from below her green eyes down her cheeks.

Óðinn! Who was this woman who dared to wear war paint in a sacred circle?

Her eyes rose to meet his.

He could hear his heart pounding in his ears as her piercing gaze held him captive. Over the years, he'd gazed into many eyes, but not ones that reminded him of the soft green moss found in the darkest corners of the forest.

Was this one of Loki's tricks?

His mind drifted, his thoughts like those of a lovesick fool, as nauseating as a skald weaving poetic verse on the virtues of the goddess Freya. It must be because he had never bedded a völva.

How would she look naked in his furs?

"Ivvár…"

Ivvár tore his gaze away. *Fool!* Even with his life and freedom in jeopardy, a woman distracted him.

A slight frown marred the king's countenance, his piercing gaze contemplating Ivvár thoughtfully before he continued. "You *will* marry."

Ivvàr glanced over his shoulder at Rorik and raised an eyebrow questioningly. There was no need for words, for they both knew marriage would destroy their bond. If he refused the punishment, the king would make him an outlaw and banish him from living among his own. Yet if he accepted, there would be children. Even though the thought did not unsettle him as much as he expected, he would not be a father that abandoned his children for long journeys, so there would be no more summer raids with his twin.

Rorik nodded at him. "You must."

He felt the noose tightening around his neck. "There will be no more raids. I lose either way."

His twin shrugged. "Your sword would be better suited for training young warriors to take your place."

Ivvár considered his brother's words. It would be a relief to stop raiding. He only went on the summer raids with Rorik to preserve the tenuous link of their twin bond. It was comforting to have a place within yourself that you shared with your twin, where you could sense each other's feelings and thoughts, where you felt whole. Rorik had turned his back on their twin bond, but Ivvár could think of nothing worse.

"I won't do it." Only in the heat of battle could he breach the fortifications Rorik used to lock him out of their bond. He needed those brief moments of closeness with Rorik on the summer raids to sustain him for the long, lonely winters. It had kept him raiding long after he was weary of the blood and death of war.

"You must, Brother," Rorik insisted.

Ivvár clenched his hands into fists, his nails digging into his palms. It mattered not whether he was outlawed or wed. Either way, he could no longer raid with Rorik, which would be fatal to their twin bond. No matter the path he chose, he would lose Rorik. An acrid taste filled his mouth. Death would be less painful than life without his twin.

King Ake cleared his throat, demanding his attention once more. "To right the wrong and mend the broken bond between our families," he said, then paused to emphasize the rest of his words. "You will marry my kin..."

Ivvàr muttered a string of curses under his breath. *Wed his kin? Surely the man jested?* He was not the first son of a reigning king, not even the first son of a jarl.

King Ake leaned back in his chair with a satisfied smile. "I have long traded with your father. It pains me that the son of Rasmus Eriksson would injure me so."

Heat burned Ivvár's cheeks. He could not deny the truth. Both his father and Valen were furious that he had slighted King Ake and jeopardized the long-standing alliance between the clans. The stern parting words flung at him as he'd boarded the longship bound for the *Thing* were to do whatever he must to make amends.

"Why wed your kin to a fourth son? I am not worthy of such *honor*," Ivvár said, the last word tasting foul in his mouth.

"Gottland is a powerful trading market. A marriage between our families will restore the bond broken by your foolishness and benefit both clans."

Ivvár heard the King's warning: accept his punishment and prosper, or deny it and all would suffer. His family and clan's fate was now entangled with his own.

"Step forward." King Ake said and motioned to the völva priestess beside him.

Ivvàr grimaced. *Was she to perform his marriage ceremony?* He had a sinking feeling that King Ake intended to shackle him in wedlock this very day.

The priestess hesitated, the heavy clay of her mask failing to hide the uneasy glance she gave the king.

Ivvár released the breath he had not realized he'd been

holding. Völva or not, there could be no wedding, for there was no bride. Many of the powerful jarls and earls that had traveled to the *Thing* were kin to the mighty king, but few brought marriageable daughters to such events. Even if there should be a suitable bride in the encampment, negotiating such alliances was a lengthy process.

"Step forward," the king repeated, brooking no argument. Red fabric swished around her legs as the völva obeyed, her wrathful countenance matching the fierce warpaint lathered over her face.

King Ake waved a hand in his direction and smiled as he spoke. "Ivvár Eriksson, meet your betrothed, my daughter, Edda."

A shocked gasp erupted from the crowd.

Nei! His stomach jumped to his throat. He could not marry her—a völva, the king's daughter.

The whites of her eyes expanded as they widened, and her mouth opened to reveal straight teeth as she gasped for air.

Ivvàr's gaze dropped to her white-knuckled hand gripping her staff, and he breathed a relieved sigh. She did not want this marriage either. He could see it in her shaky breaths and the fury that burned in her eyes like a thousand blazing suns. A marriage under such circumstances was destined to fail. He had to speak to stop this madness, now.

"King Ake, I do not wish to marry, *ever.*"

CHAPTER TWO

EDDA

arry? Her?
Everything slowed to a muted haze of shapes and dull noise. Her legs trembled. That her father even suggested such a thing showed how little he understood of her life, her calling. She was völva, healer, respected teacher of novices, and one of the few priestesses honored with being chosen to assist with the ritual sacrifices at the dísablót.

"Daughter, greet your betrothed."

Edda shook her head in disbelief. She should have known her father would do something like this, that no good would come of his summons to attend the *Thing*. He had always controlled his daughters' lives with little consideration for their wishes. Ásta, ever the good daughter, had wed the man chosen for her, who fortunately, was her childhood sweetheart. Edda had long known she would never be as good, kind, and beautiful as perfect Ásta. Eventually, her father had realized this truth too.

"Well met, Edda."

Turning her head, Edda looked at Ivvár Eriksson and ignored his greeting. She had noticed the handsome warrior as he'd waited in the crowd alongside his brother to be called to the assembly for judgment. Twin souls with red hair not dissimilar to her own were an undeniable blessing and portent of power and virility.

"Edda?" Her father's voice was heavy with that hint of warning that had successfully tempered her disobedience as a child.

But she was no child. She was a priestess, and she would not cede to any man. Edda returned her gaze to where her father sat in the highbacked chair presiding over the assembly and spoke loudly.

"Nei. I will not marry. I am völva." Inwardly she berated herself for not remaining in the secluded village where she had lived for years, inducting the newest girls into their völva training. It had been foolish to think that her father's summons for her to stand beside him at the *Thing* was his way of showing approval for her chosen path. Any other man would be proud to have a daughter dedicated to serving the gods, but not him.

Her father's fist pounded on the wooden armrest of his chair with a heavy thunk that made her jump. "This obsession with healing and magic must cease," he demanded, his voice harsh and reprimanding. "You are the daughter of a king, Edda. You will serve and honor the gods *by* marrying, just as all daughters do."

"I. Will. Not." She glared at him, fighting to restrain the magic that had swelled within her as her anger rose. "I am no longer a child whom you can intimidate and bend to your will."

"I am king," he roared. "You will do as I bid."

Her resolve hardened at his instance that she obey. "Five

summers, I have seen naught of you, and now you dare sell me off, and to a thief no less. King or not, I will not wed."

Her father's face turned a rosy shade of red, his mouth pressing into a firm line.

Edda held his gaze, refusing to back down. Her father had never had the stomach for hurting women, so there was naught he could do if she refused to cede to his foolish plan. She could not wed, ever. When a völva surrendered her innocence to a man, she would lose her connection with the gods, and that she would never allow. Her father could stomp and demand all he wanted, but he could not force the words from her mouth that would bind her to a man.

"You will wed." The steely determination in his voice sent a shiver up her spine. Had she judged him wrong? Had he changed so much these last years that he would resort to violence to force her to do his bidding?

She lowered her voice and spoke between clenched teeth. "Marriage will cost me everything, all I have worked for."

A völva without the gods was destined to slowly wither and die from losing the otherworldly bond forged through years of sacrifice and ceremony. Edda shuddered at the thought of such a fate.

"You would have me give up all I am, my life?"

"We must all sacrifice for the good of the kingdom, Edda. Ragnar Eriksson will never forgive me for outlawing his son without a blood feud. Your marriage to Ivvár will prevent war between allies. It will protect the clan, all those you love."

His words felt like a punch to the stomach. Curse him for backing her into a corner. Her uncles, cousins, and childhood friends would have to fight if she refused. The Erikssons were a powerful family, with many allies willing to fight alongside them. Even her father would struggle to find warriors willing to meet the renowned warrior sons in battle. Much blood would be spilled in a war against such a formidable army of warriors.

Snow crunched underfoot as booted feet took a step forward. "It matters not. I will not have her."

Edda looked at where Ivvár Eriksson stood with his hands on his hips, challenging her father.

He would not have *her*? The gall of the arrogant, light-fingered thief!

Currents of air eddied around her as her father rose to his feet, glaring down at the Viking warrior.

Her stomach dropped, a hard lump forming in her throat. She could feel the shift in her father's life-force, the magic that resided in all living beings, slumbering unnoticed by all except the gifted trained in the magic art of Seðir. As she watched, the slight annoyance that her father had felt with her defiance rose into the dark red thread she recognized as murderous intent. Ivvár Eriksson had pushed too far. She had often witnessed her father use the power within him, thrusting the shadowy red thread outward at those he wished to conquer.

Mayhap a father could forgive a daughter's defiance, but the king could never allow such an insult to his kin to go unchecked.

Her father bristled, his hands balling into tight fists as his body shook with unbridled rage.

Edda swallowed hard, awaiting the release of her father's wrath. Ivvár Eriksson had made a grave mistake. Even untrained in magic, her father could fell a man with the force of his wrath. She feared his power would be unstoppable on this sacred ground that held the power of the countless sacrificed to their gods.

"You *will* wed, or you will sacrifice her at the dísablót as an offering to the gods," her father roared at the Viking warrior.

"W-what?" Ivvár's face drained of color.

Her breath stilled as the full force of her father's words hit her—if she would not wed, he would have her die.

"Nei, Father." Her knees weakened under the crushing blow of his betrayal.

"You will wed or meet the gods," he interrupted in a tone that demanded obedience.

She knew that this time she would receive none of the exasperated indulgences he oft bestowed on his kin.

Slowly, he lowered himself back into his chair. "I will not be denied by either of you in this."

"Father, you know I cannot wed. I am völva," she pleaded. All she had was her calling and devotion to the gods—she could not give that up for her father, her king, or any man.

"You will do your duty…" He thrust his finger at her, his jaw tense and green eyes flashing with a dangerous warning. "Just as Ásta did."

His fury shocked her.

She could not cede.

The mention of Ásta only fed her determination. It was said that her poor sister had been forced into hiding after an ambush claimed the life of her husband and unborn child. Grieving and terrified, Ásta had suffered alone for years until she'd escaped the man hunting her and remarried. If that was the price of duty, she wanted none of it.

Edda shook her head and turned to face the man her father would have her wed.

Ivvàr Eriksson was tall and well-muscled with massive shoulders that tapered down to slim hips and long, sturdy legs.

As she had watched him approach the assembly with his

twin earlier, she had been drawn to their unusual clashing energies. She could not see the colors of their magic, for that only happened when someone lost control over their emotions, but her magic could always sense that unique life force within a being. All the twins she'd ever met had energies so bound together it was near impossible to separate, but not the Eriksson twins.

Her eyes moved over Ivvár's shoulder to where his brother stood just beyond the sacred circle of the assembly, glowering at her.

Edda pushed her magic out, seeking, and then pulled back abruptly. Rorik felt like the darkness of a wild, dangerous storm, whilst Ivvár was the quiet calm at the center. Yet sometimes, when they looked at each other, Rorik seemed lighter and Ivvár more troubled. They were a confusing puzzle, their energies broken yet still linked and influenced by the other.

"Edda?"

She glanced at her father.

He grew impatient, whisps of cold air drifting upward in white clouds when he huffed his displeasure.

Pushing aside all else, Edda returned her focus to the Viking warrior, searching for why she could argue he was not suitable. If she could just delay this foolish notion, she could make an escape.

Heat flared in the deep blue depths of his eyes at her perusal. He ran a hand through the tousled, burnt orange locks that fell over his forehead. His sun-kissed face was ruggedly handsome, and his square jaw covered in the shadow of his red beard only added to his masculine allure.

The sudden flare of heat in her chest was matched by the rosy thread of her magic shooting outwards. Her breath caught as it met his blue thread in the space between them, the two twisting around each other in a battle for dominance.

Nei!

This was not supposed to happen. She never lost control of her power and wanted none of his magic. She didn't want any husband, and certainly not a handsome one. Hurt flared deep in her chest, grounding her once more. Attractive men thought her ordinary—a painful truth she'd learned long ago. She'd thought herself in love only to discover that her suitor was using her to get close to her sister. She would not be played for a fool, not again.

Ivvàr Eriksson rocked back on his heels and crossed his arms over his broad chest until his muscles bulged in hard mounds. His gaze roamed her body as if he were assessing a breeding mare, and then his lips curved in the corners as though satisfied with her worth.

"Not him, not ever," she hissed through clenched teeth. Fury reigned as she stepped toward him. "I curse men that look at me as you do—curse them until their staff refuses to rise."

Mirth crinkled his eyes, then he threw back his head and laughed.

The mocking cadence of his amusement strengthened her resolve. She would not marry, not him, not anyone. Not even the king could supersede her vow to the gods. Death was not what she had wished, but the gods were fickle, and she would not stray from her path.

"I would rather die than wed. I shall be sacrificed to serve the gods." Her throat constricted, but she choked out the words. "You must kill me," she told the thief.

Ivvár Eriksson froze, the color leeching from his cheeks.

The crowd roared their approval, eager to see the earth stained with her blood. It had been many years since such a worthy sacrifice had been offered—the blood of a völva would surely win the favor of the All-Father and assure a plentiful harvest.

"Nei." Ivvár's gaze flicked back and forth between her and her father.

For a moment, she pitied him. It was no easy feat to take the life of one who was not an enemy, and the ritual blood-letting in the sacred grove was a heavy burden even for those men and women of magic who trained for such a purpose. A lifetime of dedication was required to learn the sacred songs and the rituals of the altar and *blót* shrine.

"It is not for you to decide, Daughter. Ivvár must choose."

Edda turned to face her father. "You need not do this. He does not want it, nor do I. Choose another punishment."

Her father waved a hand at her dismissively. "It is for the best. You will see that one day when you are surrounded by grandchildren."

"If you force me to do this, I shall never forgive you."

A moment of regret crossed her father's features before he nodded at her once and broke her heart. "So be it. I must do that which is best for the clan." His attention returned to Ivvár. "What say you?"

Her heart hammered like a sacred drum song as Edda turned to face the Viking warrior. In ritual, she loved the feeling of the tanned hide drum reverberating off her fingers and the deafening pounding in her ears. She yearned for those fleeting moments before she found the path to Yggdrasil, the tree of life that linked the nine other worlds. It was within that in-between space that she felt the full force of her connection to the gods, that she felt most alive. Her heart leaped at the thought of what that place would feel like in those moments between life and death.

Bliss.

"Sacrifice," she said, looking at Ivvár Eriksson with stead-fast determination so he would know that her decision was absolute. He was a warrior accustomed to spilling blood—he could perform the sacrifice.

Ivvár stood motionless, a momentary flare of heat in his eyes the only crack in his stern-faced expression. Yet she could feel the force of his emotions emanating in rolling waves—confusion, concern, and resignation.

Edda spoke once more, encouraging him. "Ivvár, you said yourself that you do not wish to wed. Do the sacrifice."

Ivvár glanced over his shoulder at his twin, a silent communication passing between them. Then he turned back to face her, his piercing gaze searching hers as he stroked the faint red stubble on his chin.

"Do it," she demanded.

"I'll not take an innocent life to save my own." Regret, followed by pity, filled his eyes as he shook his head. "We shall wed."

CHAPTER THREE

IVVÁR

*I*vvár traced a hand along the top of the wooden gate to the temple gardens, suddenly doubting himself for seeking solace in a place that would remind him of all he longed to forget. He looked up as the cry of an eagle rang out overhead, his gaze following the graceful flight of the predator on the hunt.

Everything had changed since he had faced the assembly of the *Thing*. He had been plagued by a constant uneasiness that made his skin prickle and left him feeling restless and awkward. And he was not awkward, ever.

He exhaled a heavy sigh as he opened the gate and stepped into the expansive fenced garden. There was no denying that he needed this, to be surrounded by plants. He closed the gate and moved along the narrow path that split the space into garden beds on one side and a large orchard on the other.

In the summer months, this garden provided both the plants used in rituals and the crops to feed the three priests of the temple and those devoted to serving them. The plentiful harvest would also be shared with all who journeyed to make an offering to the three statues of the mighty gods, Thor, Óðinn, and Freyr, who sat atop great carved thrones in the temple. But now, in late winter, the garden beds lay fallow, covered in a thick layer of snow that looked more grey than white in the gloomy light.

A soft crunch of snow underfoot echoed in the silence, capturing his attention. He veered off the path and walked toward the caped figure in the middle of a row of old apple trees. All around him, leafless branches covered in ice and snow reached outward, seeking light and sustenance.

Edda, his reluctant bride.

She leaned against a tree trunk, the green eyes that watched him matching the emerald hue of the dress she wore beneath her dark blue cape. Her hood was pulled up against the cold, one side of her face shrouded in even more shadow than that afforded by the muted winter sun.

Ivvár nodded at the two stoic warriors that hovered nearby. No doubt they were King Ake's men charged with guarding his daughter.

The warriors nodded at him respectfully and then moved away to allow them some privacy.

"Well met, Edda," he said, forcing himself to smile at his betrothed.

"Ivvár," she replied, her lips twisting sourly, as though his name tasted foul in her mouth.

"Would you like to walk?" He studied her face, curious to know the woman he would share his life with, who would choose death before marriage.

Her skin was covered in a layer of white clay, the whiteness combined with their icy surroundings making her green eyes appear brighter. Around her eyes, black kohl smudged outward to her temples and then in streaks down her cheeks.

Runes painted in delicate red lines ran from her forehead onto the bridge of her nose, the raspberry hue matching the two thick lines that started beneath her bottom lip and continued down her neck and chest.

Edda glared at him, clearly displeased with his perusal. "I wish to be alone."

He tilted his head and stared at her. He suspected she was trying to intimidate him, that she did that to men often, and it worked. Had she been interrupted? It seemed her face was painted for a ritual. Was that why she wished for solitude?

Edda pushed off the tree, scowling, her skirts brushing against his leg as she strode past him.

After motioning at the guards to follow at a distance, he fell into step beside her. She was an odd woman. Unpredictable. Mysterious. In the days since their betrothal, he'd been told that, unlike the other völva priestesses, she was never seen without her clay mask. What was the meaning of her painted face? She did not strike him as a woman prone to acting on whimsy, so it must hold some significance to her. He could not foresee what married life would be like with a wife like her at his side, but it certainly would not be dull.

"Do you enjoy apples?" he asked, motioning around them at the leafless trees decorated with shimmering icicles.

"Of course," she replied, her pace slowing when she realized he would not be deterred from enjoying her company.

"There are many apple trees in the orchard on Gottland, and plums too."

"You live on Gottland?"

"I do. Have you visited the island?"

"Nei. I have heard much talk about the trading market." Though her disposition remained frosty, her response lacked the sting of earlier.

His betrothed would be nothing like the agreeable

women who usually vied for his attentions, and he was glad
for it. His blood hummed with the thrill of the chase, a long-
forgotten feeling of excitement reigniting at the prospect of
claiming the affections of his prickly priestess bride. If they
were to be wed, and they would because he could not
murder an innocent woman, winning her affection would
make married life bearable. He was confident he could woo
her with his charm if he could keep her talking.

"I believe you will find Gottland to your liking. There is
much need for a healer and priestess in the clan."

She raised an eyebrow at him. "You assume we will wed."

"We shall." Over the last few days, he had considered
every other option, only to realize any hope of avoiding his
punishment was futile—there was no escaping this marriage.
She was fooling herself if she thought King Ake would be
swayed from this alliance to tie him to the family who
controlled one of the largest trading ports with connections
to the east.

Edda shrugged nonchalantly, but as she continued walking, the look on her face hinted that she intended to thwart
her father's plans. "Tell me of your island, Warrior. What else
grows there?"

And now she was distracting him. Clever. "There are the
fields of barley, peas, beans, and some wheat. The village
garden has carrots, onion, celery, cabbage, turnips, and many
herbs." His heart ached at the memory of the place that had
borne so many fond memories with his dearest friend.

Edda quirked an eyebrow at him as they reached the end
of the row and rounded the corner to make their way back
down another row. "How do you know so much about the
village garden?"

Pushing down the grief that threatened to overwhelm
him, Ivvár forced himself to answer. "I tended the garden

with my mentor since I was a boy." With each word he forced out, he gained a little more control over himself. The hollow ache in his chest was why he had not been back to Gottland, and why he tried not to think of Lasse, the garden, and all he had lost.

Edda slowed to a stop and looked at him, confused. "I thought all of the Eriksson sons were trained as warriors?"

"We were." A lesser man would have squirmed under her probing gaze, but he had withstood his older brother's interrogations, and naught was more frightening than the brooding Jarl's deadly stare. "But father insisted each of us also learn a trade that would help the clan in peaceful times."

"Healing plants are important for my work. Does your garden have Maegthen?"

Your garden... He supposed it was his garden now that Lasse was dead. That was certainly how the rest of the clan regarded the overgrown mess, none daring to tend to it lest they incur his wrath.

"Or Sweet Cicely?" Edda said, her breath misting in the cold.

His gaze fell to her plump pink lips and then the red lines beneath that drew one's eyes down to the slight swell of breasts hidden beneath her cape.

"Ivvár?" Her gaze narrowed, hardened at his silence.

"Já. There are many medicinal plants. Lasse spent his life creating a garden to provide for all the clan's needs." Guilt made his gut churn. All he told her was true, but he failed to mention that he had allowed the garden to fall into disarray. Or that he had been too busy using women and drink to drown his sorrows to fulfill his duty to his clan. That he no longer recognized the man he had become was a shameful truth that was hard to swallow.

Edda cupped her hands over her mouth, blew on them,

and continued her questioning, seemingly oblivious to his turmoil. "And what of Henbane and Angelica? Angelica is used often in tinctures and salves for the skin."

Walking would warm the chill from her bones, but he could not bring himself to suggest it and risk interrupting her curious questioning. "There is plentiful Angelica for your tinctures and salves. I promise."

Edda huffed in response, her misty breath curling upward over the runes painted on her nose and forehead as she waved a hand dismissively. "I shall need naught from your garden."

Ivvár took a step closer and leaned in. "I hope that is not so, Völva. I wish to share my garden and *more* with you."

Edda's eyes widened at the suggestiveness in his words. He could have sworn that their depths darkened to the same shadowed green as a forest beneath a storm cloud as her chin tilted upward, and she held his gaze with all the determination of a shieldmaiden entering battle.

"Prepare to be disappointed, Warrior."

His blood heated. Her inner fortitude appealed to the warrior in him. She would protect her young fiercely and raise strong sons and daughters. He'd not considered having children of his own, not in a long while, but now the thought pleased him. Yet, as much as he admired her strength, a part of him wanted to see her with her defenses down, to know the softer feminine parts of this fiery woman.

"Who lies beneath the fearsome völva?" Before he even realized he'd spoken, the whispered query had escaped him.

Edda froze, her slight frame stiffening. "This. Is. Me. I am völva," she ground out through clenched teeth, her tiny fist pounding her chest with each word before turning on her heel and walking away.

Ivvár watched her departure, noting her awkward jerky

gait, her clenched fists held stiffly at her sides. The hem of her blue cape swished across the frozen ground, reminding him that she was noble-born.

Little liar. Keeper of secrets.

Völva she might be, but he was no fool—that was not all there was to his betrothed.

An amused smile tugged at the corners of his mouth. He was going to unravel her secrets—every last one.

CHAPTER FOUR

EDDA

*E*dda looked up at the darkening storm clouds overhead as she stalked through the barren meadow toward her wedding. The long, dark shadows they cast matched her mood. The rising breeze on her skin and the usually soothing sensation of snow crunching beneath her booted heels fed her fury.

"Must you cover your face in that paint?" Her father shook his head at her, his long legs matching her furious pace.

"Já." Her terse response offered no further explanation nor the apology he no doubt expected. He did not understand the freedom the paint gave her—nobody did. The thick slashes of black that crossed the white clay covering her face announced to all that she was walking into battle. She wanted them to know that she was prepared to fight all of them— the curious spectators, her father, Ivvár...especially Ivvár.

"They whispered about your face in the *dísting* market," her father said, his frown deep, disappointed.

"I care naught for the loose tongues of strangers," she said bluntly. In truth, the shocked faces as she had made her way through the busy stalls toward the meadow had lifted her spirits and made her stand a little taller. That her father found it disturbing only added to her satisfaction.

"Word of your engagement to Ivvár Eriksson spread through the encampment like wildfire."

His smug tone made her bristle. His lack of fatherly consideration for her wishes was woeful. "You sound pleased."

"To join our family with one that controls the most important trading port in the region? Já. That you attend your wedding ceremony in war paint…" His nose wrinkled in disgust as his words trailed off.

"You started this *war*," she snapped, a cold chill creeping up her spine at the mention of the ceremony. Never had each stroke of the soft bristles across her face pained her more than this morn. She had been trying to run for days, each attempt foiled by the guards her father had posted. Only at daybreak, as she had spread the clay across her freshly bathed skin, had she realized that there would be no escaping this marriage.

Her father shook his head at her as though she were a petulant child throwing a tantrum. "This alliance will *stop a war* and settle the blood debt. That ugly mask will not stop me from bestowing you to Ivvár Eriksson. Nothing will halt this alliance."

Edda shook her head at him. Disgusted. "You speak of wars and blood debts, but the truth is that you traded me for coin. The paint merely reflects the death of my regard for you," she said, delivering the blow with the same deadly calm she had seen her father use against his enemies. She was his daughter, after all.

A flash of pain lit his eyes. "Danger abounds for the unwed daughter of a king. You know this, Edda. I seek to see you settled and protected. Ivvár is of a good family."

Edda shot him a scathing look. "Lies to ease your conscience." Her chest ached at the betrayal of another man, her kin. Now her only hope was that Ivvár Eriksson had changed his mind and would refuse to marry her, choosing to sacrifice her to the gods.

Her father's face was stony and resolute, no defense leaving his lips.

Edda lifted her skirts and stepped around an icy puddle. "You may have your wedding, but I will not pretend to be what I am not."

"You will do your duty?" He sounded surprised.

"You leave me little choice."

The briefest flicker of guilt darkened his eyes. "Já, Daughter. There is no escaping this fate."

"Tell yourself what you must, Father. You shall regret this day." And with those words, Edda brutally severed the thread that had bonded her with him since birth. She would never forgive him for his actions this day. He could pretend that forcing this alliance was for the clan's good, but she saw beyond the lies. The truth was that her father was an aging man in danger of losing control of his men, and he needed this alliance to hold the throne. He was vulnerable to attack or being overthrown by a greedy usurper without it.

"This is the will of the gods. You are völva—did you not ask them to reveal their will?"

"When, Father? How could I when I was followed by your warriors and had no moment alone?" Did he know naught of völva and the necessary conditions for rituals that called on the gods? She could not believe that he was so oblivious to her life, her calling, and all it entailed.

Her father waved a hand dismissively. "This marriage is the gods' will," he said. "Cease being difficult."

"Nei. It is *your* will. And you blackmailed your daughter to get it." Her blood boiled that he called her difficult because she would not eagerly agree to do his bidding. She was not pliable and obedient like Ásta—never would be.

"You have a choice."

Edda shook her head at him, astounded at how often men believed their own lies. "You threatened to cease sending the coin to the village where the völva train."

"I did."

"You know that your coin feeds the novices, that without it, they must return home to their families. You may discard my ambitions, but I will not allow you to steal those of others." Years ago, she had been naïve to believe the smooth words of a man who wanted to use her to elevate his station. Though young, she had known that her position as the king's daughter made her a target for ambitious men, yet she had never expected to be so cruelly treated. Edda knew well how one terrible mistake could steal your dreams. She would not allow that to happen to others, not without fighting back against any man attempting to crush the hopes and dreams of women for their own gain.

Her father huffed as her accusation struck.

"You began this war, Father," Edda reminded him. When Ubbe and the other boys had taunted her, she had been too young to wear war paint and fight back, but now she could. She would never be beautiful or desirable, but she was a powerful völva, and she would see that both her father and Ivvár Eriksson rued the day they forced her into this marriage. Straightening her shoulders, she closed the distance to where the small group stood, waiting for the ceremony to begin.

A murmur of hushed whispers and gasps swept through the small gathering at the sight of a bride in full war-paint.

"Come, Edda," said Alva, the high priestess who had taught her as a novice. Clad in a deep blue dress, Alva's silver hair hung loosely around her shoulders. Her left hand clutched the long steel staff said to have been forged in the fires of Múspelheim, the home of the fire giants and imbued with dwarf magic.

Edda stopped in front of her mentor, her friend. So little time had passed, yet much had changed since they'd left the village to travel to the *Thing*. She bit down on her lip to keep from begging Alva for an escape.

Alva's eyes shone with sympathy—worry lines creasing her brow.

Edda smiled reassuringly. A high priestess could not thwart the justice determined by the *Thing* assembly, not without losing her own life. And Edda refused to be the reason her völva sisters were denied a chance to train under the powerful priestess.

"I will perform the ritual," Alva said.

An image flashed in Edda's mind of her first day in the völva village, of Alva circling the fire as she spoke to the handful of new novices beginning their training.

"To be völva is to sacrifice. We give all of ourselves to heal others and honor the gods. From this day forward, your duty is to the gods. You will place none above them. The most powerful amongst us sacrifice all that it is to be a woman—they choose never to give themselves to a man, never to bear children."

"Never?" a novice asked.

"Never. Union with a man steals a völva's power and connection to the gods."

Shocked gasps that matched her own rippled through the young women sitting around the fire.

Edda blinked away the memory. She had thought little of the revelation at the time, having already given up any expectation of marriage or family. Instead, she had thrown herself into the life of völva, a life free of the bonds of man or love, until now. Now she was to marry a man that would expect her to lie with him.

Never.

She would rather be chased by the hounds of Helheim than accept that fate. Though she could not avoid this marriage, she would not sacrifice her connection to the gods for a man she barely knew, a man rumored to enjoy jumping from bed to bed.

Firming her resolve to show no weakness, Edda crossed the last few steps to stand at Ivvár's side.

"Well met, Edda," he said in greeting.

The warmth of his body heated her side, sending an uncomfortable shiver up her spine. She forced herself to remain still, not reveal how he affected her. She would show this man no weakness. Her presence would fill him with such fear that he had no choice but to back away from this reckless marriage alliance.

Something in the gleam of his eyes spoke of amusement at her painted face. It was not the reaction she'd expected. Most people responded with either shock or fear. Why was he not shocked or dismayed like her father?

"Ivvár," she replied, begrudgingly impressed at his lack of reaction to her appearance. And then she saw the curve of his knowing smile, and her stomach churned.

Infuriating man! She had seen that look before, in the eyes of a man on the hunt and excited by a challenging prey. She turned her head away, her lips pressing into a hard line. She should have known that it would take more than a painted face to intimidate this Viking warrior.

Alva began to chant, her voice ebbing and flowing over the ceremonial song.

Edda stood stiffly, keeping her gaze fixed on her friend to restrain herself from surrendering to the urge to unleash a curse on her betrothed. She was no defenseless quarry, no plaything to be toyed with to slake his loathsome need to conquer.

Ivvár shifted, bending to whisper in her ear. "What ails you?"

"Forgive me for not smiling as I am forced to marry," she hissed out of the side of her mouth.

"I too am being forced, but I shall be a good husband to you."

Her heart sank as she realized that he was resigned to this marriage.

Alva swayed back and forth, now lost in the ritual chant calling to the gods to accept the offering of fruits and mead.

Edda turned to glare at him, making no attempt to hide her fury. He denied her desire to be sacrificed, choosing to steal her control over her fate.

Unforgivable.

"Only a fool would believe a stranger." Her breath misted in the cold air, and her voice sounded harsh and heavy with disdain even to her ears.

"What of a warrior's vow? Would it ease your mind if I vowed to provide for you and that I will not seek another's bed?" His face, bronzed by wind and sun, was solemn but for the gleam of carnal promise in his eyes.

"It would not," she said, determined to rebuff his every attempt to appease her with his lies.

Ivvár turned to face her and leaned closer, his gaze holding her captive. "My parents have a good marriage, and I would have the same."

A ripple of awareness shot through her at his husky whisper.

Lifting his hand, Ivvár reached out, his fingers caressing a loose tendril of hair. "With you, I would have a real marriage. With time mayhap, there could even be love."

A real marriage? Love? They were the words of a charmer meant to soothe a reluctant bride's worries.

Ivvár grinned as he mistook her confusion for wavering resolve, his hand lingering as he tucked the hair behind her ear.

Straightening her shoulders, Edda refused to react to his touch. Her stomach clenched when her magic escaped her chest and reached for his, the shimmering threads hovering between them before she reeled hers back. The man knew he was insufferably charming and handsome and brandished it like a weapon.

"Shall I vow to protect you and take no other?"

Edda shook her head. "Nei. You must bed others," she said firmly.

Ivvár jerked backward, his easy smile disappearing as the blue thread of his magic withered to a shade of muted grey. A troubled frown notched his brows as his blue eyes studied her keenly.

"Bed others?"

Edda nodded and held his gaze, determined he would find no weakness or doubt in her manner.

A soft wind rustled the leaves at the top of the trees bordering the meadow, and Edda heard the displeased whispers of the *dísir* in the silence that stretched between her and Ivvár.

Ivvár's gaze narrowed. His voice was a hushed whisper laced with an edge of steel when he spoke. "I will *not* bed another."

Edda gazed at Ivvár—everything else, her father, the crowd, Alva, melted away. This man would be her undoing—she could feel the truth of it to her very bones.

"For us, there will be no bedding, husband. *Ever.*" Caught in the lethal calmness of his eyes, she hoped that he would hear her conviction.

Each moment felt like an eternity as his gaze refused to relinquish her, as he held her bound and breathlessly anticipating his response. *Would it work? Would he release her from this unwanted marriage? Surely he could not accept it on her terms?*

His nostrils flared, an angry black thread shooting out toward her as his mouth opened.

Edda pressed a finger to his lips. His flesh, soft yet firm, yielded to her touch most agreeably. Her breath caught. It had been many summers since she had touched a man.

Lips.

Lips were her weakness, for they could give such pleasure that even the memories of their gentle touch gave her sleepless nights.

"Liar," he whispered, his thread fading into nothingness.

Moisture coated her fingertip, his tongue sliding in a devastatingly tender caress.

Edda jerked her hand away abruptly, inwardly berating her foolishness. *Did he think her a fool?* "The sweet words that sway other women will not work on me. There will be no bedding this night or any other."

As the final notes of the ritual song echoed across the meadow, Ivvár's warm fingers wrapped around hers. A muscle in his jaw ticked as, still clutching her hand in his, he turned to face the high priestess.

Edda shifted her gaze to Alva and lifted her chin. Her words had angered Ivvár, but at least he could not claim that he did not know that his bed would be cold and lonely before they wed.

Fabric swished as Alva bent to retrieve the cup of mead placed on the stone with the other offerings for the gods, her blue dress shining lustrous against the dark skies.

Edda stilled, the hair on her arms standing on end as the crackle in the air rose with the onslaught of each bolt of lightning and growl of thunder in the distance.

Ivvár brushed his thumb across the top of her hand.

Edda released an audible breath as warmth flowed to her toes. His touch was like fire to her icy demeanor, melting her, undeniably lovely. She'd forgotten the allure of a firm calloused hand on her own and how it could make her feel—cherished, desired, protected.

Ivvár spoke in a whisper that only she could hear. "A marriage with no bedding is like a sword without a sheath."

Her blood heated. Her eyes flicked to his.

He stared at her with hooded eyes, his lips curling at the corners.

Her stomach dropped. He should be furious that she refused to bed him. Why wasn't he angry? Was that sultry gaze a promise to pursue her? She stared back at him, hoping he couldn't see her bewilderment through the clay mask.

Ivvár dipped his head, his fervent gaze dropping to her lips as he leaned closer.

Even through the paint, her lips tingled, making her want to press her fingers to them, lick them, bite them.

His words rolled off his tongue in a low, rumbled promise that sent a shiver up her spine. "No matter how long it takes, I will have you beneath me, *little wife.*"

CHAPTER FIVE

IVVÀR

*N*ightfall chased all warmth from the air as Ivvàr left the marriage feast. Ribald shouts of encouragement followed him as he crossed the field towards his waiting bride. It was time to bed his wife.

Wife.

It still felt as though this was happening to a stranger. Now that the ceremony was over, he should consider what was coming. Where would they live? His home was hardly suitable for a king's daughter.

Distracted by his thoughts, he walked toward the large tent erected a short distance from the overcrowded encampment.

Would Edda accept his kin? If this marriage had happened as a negotiation between fathers, all would have had time to get to know each other before she was foisted into his rather large and boisterous family of brothers and their wives.

Pulling back the tent flap, Ivvár exhaled heavily, resolving to do his best to shield Edda from what was bound to be persistent curiosity about his unexpected bride. All knew that he had been summoned to the *Thing*, but returning home with a wife would surely shock those that knew him best. He stepped into the warm interior and secured the tent flap before turning to survey the comforts prepared for their wedding night.

A small fire burned within a ring of stones at the center of the circular tent, sending shafts of dancing light and shadow across the furs covering the birchwood floor and the bed pressed against the far back wall. Smoke billowed through the opening at the center of the roof, curling up toward the sparkling starry sky.

Edda sat on the end of the bed in a thin white nightdress that showed the curve of her lush hips and slender waist. Her back was to him, the tips of her long auburn hair pooling around her buttocks and thighs, giving her an ethereal glow.

Edda had been unable to dissuade the women from preparing her for the marriage bed.

His lips curved into a delighted smile. If she could be persuaded to wear this sheer nightdress on her wedding night, then the seduction of his wife might not be so difficult after all.

His cock stirred, pushing against the coarse fabric of his pants, eager for release. He ached for this bedding. Since the day he had agreed to wed Edda, he'd made it known that his days of taking wayward lovers were over. He would not shame his wife by taking another. His response to her fascinated him. Over the years, he had shared furs with women but had never considered being devoted to just one. Yet here he was, not even a day married and not fazed by the thought of bedding only his wife for the rest of his days.

But Edda refused to look at him.

Ivvár turned away, allowing the tension between them to

rise. He wanted Edda a little off-balance—wariness would heighten her awareness of him. And he wanted her aware of him, his every move, every touch.

Fabric ruffled as she shifted on the bed.

She was watching him. He could feel the heat of her gaze on his back as he unfastened his furs and placed them on a hook hanging from one of the tent poles, then bent to remove his leather boots.

He'd only seen his bride that one time in the temple garden in the days before the ceremony, though he'd heard rumblings that she had tried to run. He could not blame her. He had been forced into this marriage as a punishment, but she was an innocent victim. He did not doubt that Edda believed her declaration that she would not willingly come to his bed, but he would convince her otherwise. He knew how to make a woman ache for satisfaction, to ache for him.

As he swung around to face Edda, she turned her head so that her hair shielded her face. It was just as he thought—she *had* been watching him.

"Well met, wife," he said.

"Do not call me that!" she snapped.

She was all fire and steel, his bride. She had spoken the bonding words, endured the wedding festivities with poise, and now made no attempt to hide her fury. He admired her fortitude.

"Call you what?" He crossed to the bed and placed his sword against the wall, within reaching distance as he slept. The dísablót was generally a peaceful celebration, yet one could not be too careful. He would never be caught unaware, not even on his wedding night.

Slowly, Edda stood and turned to face him. "Wife! Do not call me wife," she hissed at him.

He startled and stepped back. What in Óðinn's name had she done to her face?

The pale white clay remained in place, but she'd removed the thick dark lines of war paint worn during the ceremony. Now, two large black circles covered her eye sockets, and a slash of red surrounded her black-rimmed lips and ran down her chin like a bloody trail.

He recoiled at the gruesome sight. "By the gods, woman, you look like a corpse."

Her deep green glare was scathing. "I am dead inside."

Dead inside? Admittedly he was not the most attractive choice for a husband, given that he was not the firstborn son, but he had oft been told he was a handsome man, and there had been no complaints about his prowess between the sheets. She must not have heard the rumors.

"Surely it will not be so bad being married to me?" he said, turning to show off his best side and flexing his arms to display his muscles. Women liked that.

Her plump lips pursed in disdain as her she rolled her eyes. In a voice as dead as the markings on her face, she said, "Blessed Hel, just kill me now."

Ivvár balked at her reaction. He couldn't even remember the last time a woman had denied him.

"Remove the paint from your face, and I shall show you how alive I can make you feel," he said in the coaxing tone women found hard to resist. Unable to stop, he moved around the bed toward her.

"Nei. I will not remove it," she said and rose to her feet, her hands on her hips and jutted jaw warning that she'd not cede.

"Why not?" Stopping just a few steps from her, Ivvár reached back with one hand and pulled his shirt up and over his head. When he raised his eyes, he found her watching him, her eyes raking down over his chest and stomach to where a wispy trail of hair led down into his pants.

His blood heated at the sight of her nipples hardening into little peaks beneath the thin shift. She *was* attracted to him.

Her chest and neck flushed red, hinting at a blush hidden beneath the white clay on her face before she looked away and spoke. "This is who I am. I care not for what you think of me."

Ivvár cocked his head at her. Interesting. She was not like other women, fawning over him or seeking praise. She was unusual, a mystery he wanted to unravel.

Unravel, unwrap, and devour.

His tongue slid across his lips at the very thought of tasting her. "If you think this mask will deter me from wanting to bed you, then you are mistaken." He moved so close that his body pressed against hers, and he could taste the sweet flavor of her breath in the air between them.

"This marriage was dead before it began."

Ivvár glanced down at his groin and then back at her with a wry smile. "I am not dead."

The firelight lit the sudden beating of her pulse in her neck.

Ravishing.

"I know you do not want this marriage either," she said, her voice wavering when he advanced and pressed his thigh between her legs.

Edda stepped back and then sat on the bed.

"It is true that I had not thought to take a wife." He prowled closer and placed a knee on the bed beside her, his breeches pulling so tight across his thighs that the outline of his hard cock was visible.

Her eyes widened, and she shuffled backward across the soft furs. "Then do not do this."

Ivvár crawled toward her. "You proved your mettle by wearing the war paint to the wedding. I allowed you that victory. But here in our bedchamber, we equal."

Her eyes widened, deep green pools that followed his every move.

Good. She needed to know that he did not fear her or her magic.

"Here, there will be no defeat, only victory." He paused for effect. "Panting, shuddering, blissful victory, together."

Edda released a shaky breath.

And he knew then that he could convince her to yield. There were many ways to pleasure a woman, and he would use them all to seduce his bride.

"I cannot," Edda whispered and looked away.

Placing his hands on the bed on either side of her head, Ivvár hovered above her, careful not to scare her with the weight of his body too soon.

"What are you afraid of?"

Silence.

Edda turned her head away from him, her flaming hair covering all but the slightest glimpse of her pale soft cheek.

Slowly, Ivvár lowered himself until their chests pressed together, the lower half of his body pressed into the bed between her legs.

She stiffened and said naught. Her reaction told him that she was unclaimed and likely terrified of lying with a man. He would not take her like that—he was not a man who took pleasure in an unwilling bedmate.

Ivvár slid his hand under her cheek and gently turned her face until their eyes met. Pushing aside the frisson of heat that flooded his body, he sought to reassure her.

"You can trust me, Edda. I will make it good." He dipped his head, intent on coaxing her further with a gentle kiss.

Gasping as his lips neared, Edda arched back into the furs and turned away, her wild red curls trapped beneath her as her hand pushed against his chest.

Ivvár froze, his eyes locked on her.

"I cannot." Her voice shook as she forced the words out.

"There will only be pleasure in our bed," he promised and then shifted his weight and slid his muscular thigh against her core, providing the friction he knew would set her body alight.

Edda sucked in a shocked breath, her hands curling into fists around his shirt as her hips lifted.

His blood heated. Her words denied him, but the slight arch of her back thrusting her breasts upward betrayed the truth. Her body longed for his touch.

Edda swallowed hard, her pink lips parting and her tongue darting out to leave a glistening trail of temptation.

Gods! The honesty of her innocent reaction affected him, making him harder than tempered steel.

"Tell me you want this too," he insisted. He would hear it from her lips before he went any further. He wondered how she would taste. Sweet like fresh water on a hot day? Or intense, like the tang of exotic spices?

"Tell me." He lowered himself until his lips hovered above hers, bewitched by eyes that glowed like an emerald against the surrounding charcoal black paint.

"Nei." Her husky cry was painful, as though wrenched from the depths of her soul.

Ivvár pushed himself up and away from her. He knew some women dreaded the marriage bed, but this felt different. That wail was more than merely an objection to his presence. It was a cry of anguish, of utter despair.

A flash of steel caught his eye, and he felt a sharp prick. Clutched in her white-knuckled grip was a small dagger pressed against his stomach.

Ivvár froze, holding himself aloft and motionless as a drop of his blood slid down the tip of the blade.

"Do not touch me," Edda hissed, glaring up at him.

Ivvár made no move to take the blade from her, but neither did he back away. "You would kill me?"

Silence, accompanied by the sting of the blade pressing deeper.

He was not surprised. As völva, she would be accustomed to performing ritual sacrifices for the *blót*. Yet he was not an unwitting animal or a willing sacrifice. Threatening a warrior with a blade was dangerous. Indeed, he knew lesser men who had killed for such an insult to their pride. Was that what she wanted, for him to kill her?

"You would kill me?" he repeated.

Edda shook her head. "It is for me," she said, her tone anguished. Then her hand trembled as she turned the blade until the point pressed against her stomach.

Without a thought, his hand shot out and clamped over hers. Would she rather take her life than bed him? Why?

Gritting her teeth, Edda fought to wrestle his grip from hers. Blood dripped from his wound and seeped through the sheer fabric of her white shift.

"Stop, woman! Why do you do this?" he roared.

Her writhing stopped, her grip easing as she looked up at him with eyes filled with despair that he felt all the way to his toes.

Confident that her moment of madness had passed, he let his hand fall from hers. "Why?" he repeated, softer this time.

"My life is worthless if I am not völva."

He stared at her, baffled. "You are völva."

A heaving sigh escaped her. "Lying with a man will steal my connection with the gods. I would rather die than endure such a fate."

"But—" The hairs on his arms stood on end as he caught the renewed determination in her gaze.

Her hands thrust downward, pressing the blade toward her heart in a death blow.

Ivvár's hand shot out again, fingers wrapping around her wrist to stop the blade from finding purchase.

"Nei," she moaned.

He squeezed firmly until her hand loosened.

The blade slid onto the thick furs.

Air rushed from his lungs in a shuddering breath he hadn't realized he'd been holding. Ribs protected the heart, yet there was still a chance that the blade would have found its target.

"You will not attempt to harm yourself again. *Ever*," he growled, furious with himself for not disarming her sooner.

Edda let out a low keening whine and thrashed, her nails biting into his flesh as she clawed at him. She was a wildling, her dazed eyes and incoherent speech telling him that she was beyond reason.

Catching both her wrists, he held them above her head. He would not let her hurt herself trying to fight him. He waited, allowing her to writhe and moan beneath him as she released her fear. When her body was finally limp and her breathing slow and steady, he spoke.

"Look at me, Edda." He held her wrists firmly, unsure if she should be released.

Salty streaks stained her cheeks and the black paint around her eyes, and when her eyes lifted, the tears brimming in her lower lids glistened in the light from the burning hearth.

"I'll not be made a widower on my wedding night. You will not die."

Edda quivered at the ruthless demand. "I cannot—" Tears flowed in small streams from the corners of her eyes, wearing a trail through the charcoal paint to reveal the fragile ashen truth of the paleness underneath.

Still holding her wrists with one hand, Ivvár shifted onto the furs beside her, leaning on his side as he brushed her tears away with his thumb.

Edda watched him warily, the white clay paint and black kohl smeared across her cheek, combining into a streaky mess.

"You have naught to fear. I'll not force myself on an unwilling woman." He caressed the soft underside of her wrist as he spoke.

A sudden flash of hope flared in her eyes. "You would not?"

"Never."

"You swear?"

Ivvár stared into her eyes, his gaze steadfast as he gave her the words she needed to hear. "I swear on the All-father, I'll not bed you unless you desire it, until you willingly give all of yourself."

Drawing a deep breath through her nose, Edda sank into the soft furs, the tension easing from her limbs.

A wave of relief crashed over him. Thank the gods that he had brought her back from the edge. He released her wrists after a glance to ensure the dagger was far from reach.

Exhausted and overwrought, her head fell to the side, facing him. "And what would you ask in return?" she whispered.

Ivvár smiled, thinking about it. "I would have your vow not to curse me, little wife." He winked at her playfully. He feigned lighthearted indifference, but his heart was heavy. How had he ended up with the one woman on earth who did not want him? A völva who, in giving him her body, would lose her connection with the gods.

Her hand came up to stifle her giggles.

His grin deepened. "Swear it. Or I fear I must tickle you until I gain your promise."

Edda stared at him and then burst out laughing. "Já, *husband*. I vow these lips shall not curse you."

CHAPTER SIX

EDDA

*W*eeks later, Edda stood beside Ivvár as the longship glided toward one of the three wooden docks connecting the land to the sea. Neither the soft wind in her hair nor the calm seas could ease the rolling of her stomach as each splashing pull of oars brought her closer to her new home.

"Welcome to Gottland," Ivvár said, holding a hand to shield his eyes from the setting sun.

"It is very…busy," Edda said tactfully, watching the chaos of the small bay.

Merchants deftly glided smaller boats to and from their moored knörrs and the docks to load and unload cargo. Shouted greetings and farewells rang out from passing ships as three giant longships rowed by full crews of warriors headed out onto the open seas to keep the island's waters secure.

"Já. It is a lively port." Ivvár grinned as the shouts of men trading insults carried on the breeze.

Edda brushed stray hairs from her face. "I am just thankful that we have arrived."

"You do not like my brother's longship?"

Edda tossed him a scathing look. "Not even Óðinn himself could keep me from disembarking."

Ivvár's shoulders rose and fell as he laughed.

"It is not amusing. I swear the goddess Rán was taunting me with that storm." Edda shuddered at the thought of the long journey huddled in the tent Ivvàr had erected in the center of the deck, too sick to move. "Thank the gods, it is over."

Ivvár's eyes crinkled at the corners as he shook his head at her. "It was just a small squall."

Edda huffed in disagreement. "You weren't hanging over the side emptying your stomach into the sea for days."

"It is true that you do not have sea legs, little wife."

Edda ignored the endearment. Ivvár had proven himself a man of his word and had made no further attempts to bed her, and so, in return, she overlooked his teasing. Her gaze moved to the shoreline of the sandy bay.

"Viking raiders can have the seas. I need to feel the earth between my toes." Fortunately, the warmer weather had chased away the winter chill on their journey, and the first signs of spring could be heard in the forests and felt in the sea air. Notwithstanding an unexpected late-winter storm, she could soon kick off her boots and go barefoot.

She swayed with the movement of the deck as the longship bumped against the dock.

The ropes were thrown and tied off.

Warriors leaped onto the dock, greeting their wives and boisterous children.

Her hand rose to her chest at the sudden sharp pain she

felt inside. Once, long ago, she was waiting on the dock for her father to return from battle or trading journeys. Yet that feeling of joy she could see on the faces of these reunited families had deserted her many years ago when she'd lost her sister and left her father in the same summer to train as völva.

The crowds on the dock parted for a tall warrior with long golden hair hanging loose around his shoulders.

"Well met, brother," the warrior greeted.

Edda glanced at the rolled-up sleeves of his shirt and the inked markings covering his forearms, then up to his piercing blue eyes that studied her. The warrior's expression remained unmoved, but his eyes narrowed with curiosity as he saw her painted face.

"Valen!" Ivvàr leaped from where he stood beside her onto the dock and pulled his brother into a back-slapping embrace.

Valen. This was the Jarl of Gottland, leader of the Eriksson clan. He was just as Ivvár had described—older, wary, stern.

Valen returned Ivvár's embrace.

Edda hid her surprise at the genuine affection between the brothers. After the long, tense journey back to Gottland with Rorik and Ivvár, she'd expected discord between all nine of the Eriksson brothers. Yet it was clear that the bond between these two was strong.

Her gaze moved to the slender dark-haired woman standing behind Valen, clutching a small wriggling child in her arms.

Samara.

The lovely cadence of her name matched the glowing beauty of the Arabian princess that Ivvár spoke of often. Six summers past, the Eriksson Jarl's choice of bride had caused scandal and jealousy amongst the families who lamented the loss of such a powerful and wealthy potential husband for their daughters.

Edda smiled gently and then waited for Samara to flinch or startle at the sight of her. She was accustomed to people fearing her painted face. Edda cursed herself inwardly for choosing the likeness of a wolf for this important day. She didn't want to be feared by those she would live amongst, mayhap by the men, but not the women and children. Her friendships with women she had considered sisters had seen her through völva training and then the grief of losing Ásta, followed by the shock of learning her sister lived. But now, her völva sisters were across the sea in their village, and she was alone.

Samara tilted her head, her amber eyes narrowing, assessing.

Edda waited. To survive in this new clan, she would need to forge new bonds with the women here, especially the Jarl's wife.

Samara nodded once, a silent acknowledgment before she smiled back.

Edda released the breath she'd been holding—hopeful that having avoided outright rejection for her unusual look meant she would soon befriend the Jarl's wife.

"Edda?" Ivvár leaned over the side of the longship with his arm outstretched, offering her his hand.

Suddenly nervous, Edda slid her hand into his. She often traveled with Alva to tell fortunes and heal, but this was different. Gottland was to be her home, and she wanted this introduction to go well. Ivvár's firm grip gave her the courage to step onto the dock with her head held high, but then she swayed. Her legs felt wobbly, odd, and the morning meal threatened to come back up.

"Careful, you have sea legs. It will soon ease." Ivvár's hand remained wrapped around hers, his other cupping beneath her other elbow, supporting her.

"Gods…" she whispered. Would the torture of the seas never end?

"Close your eyes and breathe."

Edda did as he bid, sucking deep, shuddering breaths into her lungs. Her shakiness receded, taking with it her courage. With eyes closed—she was aware of every brush of his fingers against hers, his heady scent, laced with the hazelnuts they had shared earlier, surrounding her.

Dangerous.

Forcing her eyes open, she turned to face the Jarl. Everything within her longed to wrench her hand away, but she could not shame Ivvár in the presence of his family.

"Valen, Samara, this is Edda. My wife."

Valen's furrowed brow twitched, an almost imperceptible sign that he was shocked at Ivvár's revelation.

"Edda, this is my brother, Jarl Valen Eriksson."

"Your wife?"

A chill started in her chest and spread to her toes. Gods, the Jarl was looking at her as though she were a *Draugr*, one of the undead returned to haunt his family—this was not a fortuitous beginning.

"Já. I am wed. King Ake demanded a union between our families to right the wrong done to him. Edda is his youngest daughter."

"I see." Valen gave Ivvár a solemn nod, his harsh countenance easing as he pulled his wife and child into his arms.

Edda watched his dark blueberry thread unfurl from his chest to twine and dance with the brilliant yellow of his wife's as she looked up at him adoringly. Undeniably, they shared a love bond.

BEWITCHED VIKING | 55

"Welcome, Edda," the Jarl continued. "Blessings on your marriage. This is our son, Brandr. You are völva?"

"I am."

"Samara is with child. I welcome the arrival of a healer to our clan."

"Gratitude." Edda smiled and inclined her head. "It would be an honor to attend your wife for the birthing."

"You are Ásta's sister?" Samara tilted her head to the side thoughtfully as she spoke, her long dark tresses falling forward into the eager clutches of her son.

"I am."

Samara smiled brightly, prying her hair from the boy's chubby fist. "Your sister was very kind when I arrived here alone and afraid. I am gladdened that I may repay her kindness to her kin.

Edda lowered her head respectfully. "I would like that too."

Ivvár's hand squeezed hers, a pleased smile on his handsome face. "My wife is weary, brother. I would have her rest."

Edda nodded in agreement. "It was a long journey, and I was not well."

"The seasickness?" Valen asked.

Ivvár nodded and then bumped her shoulder with his playfully. "Most days, she violently emptied her stomach over the side."

"From the shock of those on board, you would think they had never seen a sick woman," she shot back.

Ivvár laughed aloud. "They merely expected the daughter of the infamous Viking raider Ake Sorensen to be born to seas."

Edda shook her head. It seemed she could not escape her father or being cast as the unbefitting daughter, even far from his court. "I never had cause to journey beyond my father's lands. This was the first time I had been on the open seas."

"You did well, wife." Ivvár smiled down at her.

A flush of warmth spread through her at his compliment. "I think the men would disagree. Especially those groaning each time I retched, and then louder when the contents of my stomach slid across the deck near their feet."

Samara laughed. "It is fortunate you had Ivvár to care for you."

Edda nodded, although she was still struggling to understand the motives behind his kindness. Not once had he complained or chastised her for being sick. Instead, he'd brought her water and food, patiently coaxing her to eat despite her protests that she would bring it back up. And when she could not move, he'd remained at her side, pressing a cool cloth to the back of her neck as he told her tales of his family and childhood in Gottland.

Samara placed the wriggling little boy in her arms on the ground. "Valen. You must tell Ivvár of the trouble with the mice in the fields."

The Jarl nodded at Ivvár. "Já. Old man Jorik lost a third of the barley he planted in his north paddock."

"Edda. Your cat."

Edda startled and then turned toward the gruff voice.

Rorik stood on the longship deck with his arms crossed over his chest, scowling up at her.

Pity twisted her insides. There was a sadness in her husband, but not the darkness that haunted his twin.

"Your cat," Rorik repeated in a tone as stern as his handsome features. He looked pointedly at the wooden cage he had placed on the dock at her feet and then back up at her.

Edda glanced at Ivvár. He was still speaking with Valen

bout mice and crops. She pulled her hand free and crouched down to look through the wooden bars.

Sól was curled up inside his cage, his head resting on his paws as he waited to be conveyed to his next home. She'd been just a child of eight summers when her father gifted her the longhaired forest kitten after a trading journey far to the east of his lands. He'd said it was the sunset orange fur that matched the hair on his youngest daughter's head that had convinced him that she and the creature were fated to belong to each other. Now she knew that Söl was a gift from the goddess Freya who had bestowed the gift of seiðr to the world and rides in a chariot pulled by two giant cats that are her constant companions.

"Sweet Sól."

Sól purred, not bothering even to lift his head in greeting. As a kitten, he had followed her around like a shadow, but nowadays, he was content to spend his days lying in the sun or jumping out of trees and startling unsuspecting passersby.

"My thanks, Rorik," she said, not expecting a reply. Rorik rarely spoke. Nor did he attempt to hide the heavy darkness within him from his expression. Unease had coursed through her body the first time she met Rorik and saw the dark grey magic that swirled around him. She had wondered if he was sick of the mind, a madman that took pleasure in harm and destruction. But then Rorik had looked at Ivvár, his grey flashing deep red before fading back to grey, and she'd known she was wrong. It was a glimpse of another man hidden beneath all the scowling silence. Her suspicions were confirmed a few days later, after what felt like endless purging over the side of the longship.

She woke to his frowning face looking down at her as he brushed the hair from her eyes.

Alarmed, she struggled to sit upright.

"Lay still," *Rorik demanded in a tone that brooked no argument.*

"*I must—*"

"*You must rest. I will tend to the anima.*" *His dark gaze avoided hers as he pushed her firmly back into the furs. His kindness caused naught but the tiniest glimmer of light in the gray that surrounded him, but she knew then that there was hope for the man whose thirst for violence and blood was spoken of in hushed whispers by even the most formidable warriors—he had not yet surrendered to the darkness.*

Unperturbed by his gruff bearing, Edda gave Rorik a soft smile. "You have cared for Sól well." She would not forget his kindness to her furry friend—it was a debt she was determined to repay.

Rorik grunted in response and stepped onto the dock. "He needs to be fed." He delivered the words in a sharp bark punctuated by a finality that laid to rest any further discussion.

"My thanks, Rorik."

Scowl deepening, Rorik turned on his heel. The wooden planks shook underfoot as he stomped toward the beach without greeting his kin.

"He is as sour as ever." Worry marred the Jarl's features as he watched Rorik stride up the foreshore.

Ivvár sighed. "Já. Sour and secretive." Hurt flashed across his face before he bent to pick up the wooden cage containing Sól. "I would get my wife home now. Will you have some food sent and her chests delivered?"

Valen nodded and moved aside to allow them to pass. "It will be done. Rest well. I shall tell mother and father that you have retired early, but they will be impatient to meet your new bride in the morn."

"I would like that," Edda said. The last time she had seen

Jarl Rásmus and his wife, Drifa, was at Ásta's wedding to
King Njal Helgesen. Still just a child, she had been more
concerned with thoughts of Ubbe than aiding her sister's
marriage preparations with the other women.

"Come, Edda." Ivvár's arm wrapped around her shoulders, sending heat surging through her body as he led her
along the dock and onto the beach.

Edda waited until they reached the towering stone wall
surrounding the town before she stepped out of his grasp.

"Stop touching me. I do not want your hands on me." She
needed to stop this overfamiliarity. On the longship, she had
become far too accustomed to his touch.

Ivvár cocked his head and considered her. "Is it my touch,
or that you enjoy it, that bothers you?"

"Now that we are at your home, we will lead separate
lives just as agreed," she said. She purposely avoided his
question, not wanting to confirm his suspicion lest he use it
to justify pursuing her further.

"Is that so?" Ivvár turned and walked away. "Then I shall
show you your new home," he tossed over his shoulder.

Edda hurried to close the distance between them as Ivvár
rounded a corner and strode through a busy marketplace,
waving and smiling broadly at those that welcomed him
home.

Walking alongside, Edda watched in amusement as
passersby recognized her as völva and lowered their eyes or
nodded respectfully. The crowds thinned as they left behind
the market and trade workshops to walk along a wide path
between rows of small wooden cottages with thatched
rooves.

"Is Visby a large village?"

"Já. Many families who farm the land live outside the

walls, and those who live inside the walls are too many for longhouses."

"There are no longhouses?"

"Just one for the Jarl and his family. My father had cottages built for everyone else."

"For so many?"

Ivvár nodded. "It took many summers, but now we only add one or two each summer for newlyweds."

"We will have our own home?" She had never heard of such a thing. Even her father's people still shared longhouses. Such was the Viking way.

"Já. We do."

Uneasiness made her skin prickle. She had prepared herself to share a longhouse with others, finding comfort in knowing there would be few opportunities for privacy. Now she was walking toward a house she would share with Ivvár alone. Would he keep his vow not to violate her?

"What of the animals? Where do they live if no longhouse has a place to house them over the cold winters?"

"There are two shared animal houses with bedchambers for the unwed warriors that care for them in the winters."

"Oh." The last glimmer of hope that she would not be alone with Ivvár disappeared as the whisper escaped her. She supposed it mattered not, Ivvár had vowed not to force her, and she did believe he would honor his word. They would live as strangers, separate lives with paths that rarely crossed. Surely it would not be so hard?

Ivvár pointed at a large building, its thatched roof towering above the others. "That is the Great Hall, and Valen's longhouse is beyond..."

"You have a hall just for feasting?" Edda glanced at the massive Great Hall, a long wood and stone structure that would have rivaled even one of her father's buildings. So many thatched cottages and now the Great Hall left no doubt that this family was wealthy from the prosperous trading market.

"Já. Father had the hall built."

"And what is that?" Edda craned her neck to see behind the small well to the thicket of green.

"That is the garden," Ivvár said sharply and quickened his pace.

Edda started at the sudden snappish turn in his voice. *Had she offended?* Hastening after him, Edda glanced at the thick greenery visible over the top of the rock wall surrounding the garden. "This mess is the village garden you spoke of?"

"Já."

"But it is so overgrown. Those apple trees look like they have not been pruned in years."

"As everyone keeps reminding me," Ivvár muttered and then seized her hand and tugged her impatiently across the wide lawn ringed by blossoming apple trees.

"Are the beds inside barren and neglected too? You promised me angelica grew in the garden. If I had known otherwise, I would have brought seeds for planting."

"It is in there," Ivvár said somewhat shamefacedly.

"Not anywhere it can be found. You best fix that garden, Ivvár. I must have that angelica for my healing work, and I do not wish to ask the other women in the village to share theirs."

"I keep my word. You shall have all the angelica you need."

Edda huffed at his back as he walked off, pulling her along behind. "Why does everyone trouble you about the garden?" She was forced almost to a run to match his brisk pace.

"It is not your concern," he said, his voice firm, final.

Edda pried her hand from his. "You walk too fast."

Ivvár huffed but then continued somewhat slower.

Edda stared at his broad shoulders as she followed him silently along the well-trodden dusty path, quelling the urge to probe further. The only other time she'd seen Ivvár so bothered was when she'd seen the heaviness that clung to the air when he stood with Rorik, and she'd realized that something was broken between the brothers. To know how to keep the warrior from seeking her bed, she needed to understand the man with whom her life was now entwined. She would study him with the same devotion she had applied as a new novice to learning the plants and brews used in healing. First, she would discover the cause of the rift between the brothers, and then why mentioning the garden upset her husband.

Ivvàr slowed to a stop and pushed open the rickety gate to a small rectangular stone cottage with a weathered wooden roof.

Her heart sank. She stared at the gaps in the rough timber fence that ran along both sides of the home and the rotting timber poultry house that tilted dangerously.

Blessed Freya, please let it not be worse inside. She had little hope that the goddess would hear her plea, yet she had to try, for she suspected that the cottage was not fit for a hog shelter.

"This is your home?" Try as she might, she could not hide her disappointment. This unkept cottage was even further from her royal chamber than the small hut she'd shared with the novices.

"Já. I have been away much, so there is a need for repairs." Ivvàr marched to the door, Sól's cage swinging back and forth in his left hand.

Repairs? He needed a new house. And she needed a

moment to gather herself after the shock. "I need to relieve myself."

Ivvár halted in the doorway. "It is around back with the bathhouse."

"You have a bathhouse?"

"Já. It is filled by hot water diverted from the hot spring that runs along the back of all the cottages this side of the Great Hall."

"That is an uncommon luxury even for the son of a Jarl."

Ivvár looked at her and raised his eyebrow suggestively. "I like to bathe. I want to bathe you too, wife." Chuckling at her shocked silence, Ivvár turned and disappeared inside.

Edda made her way to the back of the cottage. Somehow the garden was even worse there—a wild mess of brambles and shrubs that she weaved through to reach the outhouse.

"Ugh." Edda gagged on the overwhelming stench as she closed the door and lifted her skirts.

He is a stranger. The thought was another in a growing list of reasons to stay away from Ivvár. He was a stranger with secrets, an appetite for jumping from woman to woman and using his charm to get his way.

Not with her.

Ivvár was a warrior accustomed to chasing the thrill of conquest. Surrendering to him would not end well—after the joy of the chase wore off, her handsome husband would tire of her and seek his pleasures elsewhere. And she would be alone. Alone and abandoned by both her husband and the gods.

Edda released a slow breath. There would be no surrender, not while she breathed.

After tending to her needs, Edda returned to the front of the cottage and paused on the doorstep.

You can do this. This is your home now.

She would build a life here, offering blessings to the gods for the Eriksson Jarl and healing the villagers whilst Ivvár raided and sought his pleasures elsewhere. Straightening her shoulders, she pushed open the oak door and crossed the threshold.

"Ivvár?" Edda stepped into the musty room, her boots scuffing across a pebble in the dark. As her eyes adjusted to the dim light shining through the doorway, she could see the faint outlines of the sparse furnishings. The cooking area was little more than a long timber counter for preparing food and a small hearth beneath an opening at the center of the roof to let the smoke escape.

"Stay there. I will light the fire." Even in the darkness, she could see the clouds of dust billowing as Ivvár crossed to the hearth marked by large stones placed in a circle. His shadowy figure was barely visible as he removed the metal frame that had a large chain with a hook dangling over the spent ashes.

Edda covered her nose to keep from sneezing. With only a door to let in natural light, the insides of longhouses and cottages were dark even during the day. She would be glad for the light cast by a fire.

The scratch of flint hitting a fire-steel echoed in the quiet. Sparks illuminated the sharp lines of her husband's profile as flames burst to life. The outline of his broad shoulders strained against the fabric of his dark blue tunic and the stiffness in his back and shoulders.

After Ivvár lit a small lantern and placed it on the simple wooden counter to her left, Edda scanned the small cottage, now lit by a soft glow. Beyond the central hearth sat a small table and two chairs, and behind a large tapestry suspended from the roof, she glimpsed a wooden bed on stilts.

"Apologies that it is so dusty. I was not expecting company." Ivvár opened the wooden cage and pulled Sól out. His large hand brushed over her cat's fur, his long fingers lingering on the fluffy tail until Sól protested and was placed on the floor. "This was my mentor's home. I rarely sleep here."

"Because you were too busy jumping from bed to bed." The words were out before she even realized she had spoken.

"Já. Edda, I will never lie to you. I was not lacking for bedmates, but those days are behind me now."

"I certainly hope not." Better he sought another's bed than her own.

Ignoring her jibe, Ivvár pulled some dried cod from a pouch at his waist and tossed it in a bowl. "I hope you will be comfortable here."

Not likely. She doubted she would ever feel at ease in this home with him.

After pulling the stopper from his bladder, Ivvár added a little water to soften the dried cod before placing the bowl on the floor. "That should satisfy your cat until morning."

"Gratitude. It has been a long journey for Söl."

"We should get to bed. It will be a busy morn."

"Já. There is much to set to rights here." Edda looked around, assessing the task ahead. "Mayhap more than a few days of work. At least I must not sleep on the floor with those mice," she said, pointing at the messy nest in the corner of the room.

For a moment, Ivvár looked sheepish, apologetic even. "Let's go to bed." He lifted the lantern and moved to the tapestry.

"And where shall you sleep?" she said as she followed.

"We share the bed." Ivvár looked over his shoulder, the firelight flickering over the angular line of his jaw.

Her heart skipped a crucial beat, and her breath lodged in

her throat. "I cannot." This was not happening. He had given his word. The room spun, making her stomach heave. Stray hairs flicked across her cheeks as she shook her head, beseeching him with her eyes to understand. "Lying with a man will rob me of my power."

Ivvár turned to face her, his eyes narrowing. "You said *bedding* a man would steal your power."

"It is the same thing," she huffed, placing her hands on her hips and glaring at him.

"Nei, it is not," Ivvár growled. "If I cannot pleasure my wife, then by Óðinn, I will share a bed with her." His eyes darkened, intense and unwavering, as he held her gaze.

A lump caught in her throat. For the first time, she felt alone—no family, no Alva, no sisters in magic. She was at war with a stranger, on enemy territory, and exhausted. She was fighting a losing battle—on this, Ivvár was determined to have his way.

An uneasy silence settled between them.

"I cannot." The last thing she wanted was to share furs with any man, especially him.

"You can," Ivvár growled and pulled back the draped tapestry.

Infuriating man! Her hands clenched into tight fists at her sides.

Choose wisely when to fight and when to retreat.

Learn the enemy. Study him.

And then beat him.

With her father's words ringing in her mind, Edda moved past Ivvár and into the bedchamber.

The room was small, with three rough timber walls and an earthen floor. An imposing carved oak bed dominated the room, and a large carved chest was pushed up against the end.

"It is simple but comfortable."

Edda's gaze fell to the worn timber chair at the far end of the room. Carvings of the All-Father peeked out beneath the clothes thrown haphazardly across the backrest. Beside it, a narrow table and stool had been pushed up against the wall and into the corner. Only a man would think this messy, unkempt chamber comfortable.

After setting the lantern on the bench, Ivvár hastily tugged the musty blankets from the bed and tossed them in a corner before opening the chest. He lifted a mass of furs and blankets and spread them across the large bed.

"In the morn, I will replace the straw."

Edda nodded awkwardly. This house, being here with him, felt…unsettling. What had her father been thinking? There were never two people so different and ill-matched as she and Ivvár—this marriage was destined to end in disaster.

"I will leave you to undress." Ivvár dropped the tapestry back in place, and she heard his footsteps moving away.

Relieved, Edda placed her pack on the narrow bench beside the lantern. She longed to curl up and sleep until dawn, but her frayed nerves would never allow it. After casting one last look at the bed, she turned away.

"Unpack and then sleep later," she muttered. Much later —when she was assured that Ivvár slumbered. Tugging on the laces at the front of her gown, she carefully stepped out of it and lay it across the back of the chair with the other discarded clothing. Slowly, she unwrapped her glass jars of clays, powders, and kohl, arranging them neatly at one end of the bench.

"Now you are home." She felt better just seeing the precious clays that hid her face from the world. Next came the small package wrapped in soft skins in the bottom of her pack. Carefully, she unwrapped the tanned hides that protected her mirror. It was an expensive extravagance, the first thing she had traded for when she began to receive coin in payment for her tinctures and balms. Lifting the small square of glass backed with tin purchased from a trader from the lands far to the east, Edda studied her reflection.

Hideous Edda.

The jeering taunts of Ubbe and the other young warriors had followed her for years after that fateful day he had rejected her. Ubbe had encouraged them to be merciless and had enjoyed watching her suffering.

Hideous Edda.

The sly barb, spoken only when they were out of earshot of her father or any other who would defend her, hurt just as much as the stones they threw as she'd walked alone in the forest. She had cried, begged, and pleaded as they'd laughed in her face and continued their ruthless campaign.

Until she became völva.

The first day she had donned the crimson dress of a priestess and the mask of a wolf, everything had changed. One glance at her painted face and her tormentors had averted their eyes and backed away respectfully. The mask made her powerful, but without it, she reverted to the same unsightly girl as before.

Hideous Edda.

Not even the wolfish features she had painted on this morn could hide her faults. There was naught appealing about her whatsoever. Sighing heavily, she set down the glass on the tanned hide wrapping. She preferred to remove the clay and reapply it in the morning, but that would not be possible now that she would be sharing the bedchamber with Ivvár.

Ivvár.

Every part of her rioted at the thought of sleeping beside

him. They'd had constant company on the ship, but now he had her alone in his home...

Satisfied that her mask had not worn off, she moved swiftly to the bed. Better to be hidden from view when he arrived. Her fingers lingered on the bedding as she pulled it back, glad for the softer linen fabric beneath that would shield her skin from the coarse woolen blanket beneath the layer of thick furs. Laying down, she pulled the bedding over herself and faced the wall.

The smell of man invaded her nostrils—earthy, musky, delicious. Dangerous. There was no escaping Ivvár's overwhelming presence, even in this rarely used bed. Her chest tightened at the thought of sleeping beside her large brawny husband. Would she feel the heat of his body? *Nei!* She rolled onto her back, determined to ignore the sudden tingle between her legs. The touch of the furs against her arms and neck sent a shiver racing up her spine. Her breath was coming quicker now, and she could feel her magic vibrating, surging toward a release, uncontrollable.

Calm yourself. Alva's stern demand rang loud over the racing thoughts and panic clouding her mind.

Edda stared at the ceiling as she tugged at the leather tie around her neck and pulled the carved bone pendant from beneath her shift.

Be. Calm.

Earthing, finding balance, and cultivating a peaceful mind were the first skills new novices mastered. Reciting one of the simpler chants in her mind, Edda fingered Freya's rendering. The words flowed through her mind, the familiar ebb and flow of their cadence, a soothing rhythm that soon eased the tightness in her chest.

A whoosh of air caressed her face as the tapestry moved and then fell back into place.

Ivvár had returned.

She lay still as his gaze roamed over the outline of her figure hidden beneath the covers. Her breath caught at the wolfish hunger in his eyes. All that stood between her and ruin was honor, his honor. After a lifetime protected by her father and then the high priestess, she loathed that she was now vulnerable, that her fate rested with another. There was naught she could do but hope that he would keep his vow.

As though sensing her discomfort, Ivvár crossed to the chair. Facing away from her, he pulled his shirt over his head. The lantern cast flickering golden light and shadow patterns across his tanned skin, over his broad, muscular shoulders and back.

That throb between her thighs returned. After many summers living in the forest with naught but other women novices, she had forgotten the alluring sight of a man unclothed.

Ivvár moved to unfasten his pants.

A whimper escaped her.

His hands stilled. Twisting at the waist, Ivvár looked over his shoulder at her. A smile tugged at the corner of his mouth.

"Do you like what you see, little wife?" he teased.

Edda shook her head and licked her dry lips. "N-nei." It was a blatant lie, a necessary lie. His bare flesh brought up feelings she had long forgotten existed within her.

Lifting the lantern, Ivvár moved toward the bed, his unhurried stride reminding her of the prowling gait of a predator on the hunt.

Her heart hammered in her chest. It took all her self-control to hold fast to her magic and restrain her surging energy until it settled.

"You are a terrible liar, Edda." Ivvár placed the lantern on the floor, his eyes twinkling with mirth as he sat beside her.

Her fingers curled into the thick furs at the sudden dip of the bed. "I am not," she protested, though her words rang untrue even to her own ears.

"You are. As I would be, were I to claim I did not want to ravish you."

"Ohh," Edda spluttered, dumbfounded by the sudden rush that ignited in her veins with the same fury as Thor striking Mjölnir and setting the skies ablaze.

Ivvár removed his boots, each falling to the floor with a heavy thud.

Gods! Would he remove his pants? Was she to face the sight of her husband in all his naked glory?

He dimmed the lantern and slid in beside her.

Until her eyes adjusted to the muted light, Edda lay motionless, his scent overwhelming her as much as the heat of his body radiating against her side.

At least he is not naked.

And then he rolled to face her and reached out.

Sweet Freya! Her heart lurched at the tender brush of his fingers trailing down her arm.

"Come closer, wife," he said in a low husky whisper that could have tempted even the dwarves of Svartálfheim to share their treasures.

Nei! *Hold fast and resist.*

His hand slid beneath the furs and across the front of her shift before tenderly cupping the swell of her breast.

Her pulse skittered wildly. She was adrift, rudderless, but for the fervent, aching need.

"Gods, I burn for you." His thumb brushed across her nipple.

Edda jolted at the surge of pleasure that raced through her body, the seductive haze he had cast over her fading.

"Nei." She shoved his hand away. It was unfair that his hands made her feel like ice melting on a warm day. She had forgotten that he could play a woman's body with the same masterful confidence as an accomplished bard playing the lute. She would not allow him to use that knowledge against her to slake his own needs.

"What is wrong?" he whispered.

"I would hold you to your word—there will be no bedding," she demanded, as dread stole her breath and forced her to wait for his response. Would he lash out at being denied? Women often spoke of the violence of those men who returned from raiding accustomed to taking women by force. Was he such a man?

Silence followed her demand—heart-stopping silence.

"I would have the truth, Ivvár. Am I to be abused and violated by my husband?"

Ivvár rested his head on his hand and looked down at her, his affront obvious. "I would not hurt you, ever."

"But…." She was glad of the shadows that hid the heated flush in her cheeks. "You touched me as…"

"As a man touches his wife?"

"Já." She was relieved that he spoke the words that she could not.

"I vowed there would be no bedding if you did not desire it, Edda. I *never* promised not to seduce you."

Her gasp sounded like a clap of thunder in the silent room. Her mind recalled their wedding night and his exact words. He spoke the truth—his vow did not exclude him from seducing her.

"You used slight of words, so I would think myself safe from your attentions."

He shrugged, not in the slightest apologetic. "You attacked me with a blade and were terrified. I did what I must to calm you."

"You tricked me. All along, you planned to seduce me."

His lips curved into a coy smile. "I hoped that you would come to know me and mayhap the thought of bedding me and having children would not be so loathsome."

Gods, she was a fool. "You know the stakes if I yield my body. Do not attempt to convince me that a night with you is worth more than honoring the gods." Edda shook her head at him. "I should have known not to trust a man renowned for wooing women."

"Come now—"

"Do not insult me by denying it," she spat at him. "You'll not find me so willing as your past conquests, husband. Indeed, you will not find me willing at all." Edda rolled away from him, furious at herself for letting him play her false.

"You protest like one struggling to resist, little wife."

Edda froze as one lone finger pressed against her nightdress and trailed languidly down her spine to the indent above her bottom. Her skin burned hot where he touched her, his finger hesitating tantalizingly over the hollow cleft. She could not breathe, or think.

"Are you already falling under my spell?" Ivvár whispered with the conviction of a man assured of the effect of his ministrations.

When his hot breath caressed her ear, Edda knew that the delicious warm shiver that wracked her body was no mistake. Ivvár wanted to bed her, intended to claim her. His every touch was his war cry, his declaration of his intent to claim her as his prize. To him, she was but a conquest.

Suddenly, she was back in the forest, surrounded by darkness and engulfed by a bitter cold numbness. That was how her father's men had found her, rocking back and forth, lost even to herself, as Ubbe's words repeated in her head.

"Did you think I wanted you, that anyone would want you?" An ugly sneer accompanied the words.

"You said you loved me."

"I lied." Ubbe threw back his head and laughed at her distress. *"Hideous, foolish girl. I courted you to get close to Ásta. Her beauty shines like a rare gem, and yours like a muddy river stone. I would never want you."*

"Hideous Edda."

Ubbe turned to the friend that had spoken. *"Já, Kavi. She is hideous Edda."*

"But... I-I love you."

Kavi laughed. *"Mayhap you should take the hideous princess for your wife, Ubbe,"* he said teasingly, making the other young warriors at the table snicker.

Ubbe's gaze returned to hers, fury raging in the light blue depths she so adored.

Her heart dropped, and she stumbled back a step. He was furious that he had lost his chance with Ásta, and now she had embarrassed him in front of his friends. The last was a grave mistake. Not only had she shamed him, but she had made him a target too. Unforgivable.

"You shall be known as hideous Edda," Ubbe said with the confidence of a man that knew his word would be law to those that followed him. She had shamed him, and this was her punishment.

She was ruined. And so she ran.

"Sleep well."

The rumble of Ivvár's satisfied tone pulled Edda from her memories. Her husband did not know it yet, but she would not be so easily won. She had fled into the forest after Ubbe's rejection, deep into the wilds of her father's lands. There was little she remembered of the time she was missing, but Ásta later told her that it was three days before she was found shivering and parched in the hollow of an oak tree and carried her back to her father. Those days lost in the forest, alone and heartbroken, had broken her. The scars over that wound were strong, impenetrable. Wide awake, Edda gazed into the darkness until Ivvár's breathing slowed.

Nevermore will I allow a man to hurt me.

She would not break the vow she had made while alone in that forest. Not for him, not for anyone.

Ever.

CHAPTER SEVEN

IVVÁR

*I*vvár shifted his chair to catch the cool night air flowing through the open doors. The slight breeze provided a welcome respite from the heat of the crowded Great Hall. The din of the boisterous clan was overwhelming after so long away raiding and fighting with just a few warriors for company. He had been back on the island for three days and longed to escape company for a quiet corner. He drained his mug and slammed it on the table, welcoming the burn of tart ale in his throat.

"Thirsty, brother?" Rorik quirked an eyebrow at him, then lifted the pitcher and refilled his mug.

"Returning to clan life is better borne drowned in ale." Ivvár leaned back in his chair and scanned the hall until his gaze fell on his wife sitting across the room talking with Samara. His eyes roamed up and down, taking in the swell of her breasts beneath the moss green apron dress and the gentle curves of her hips in the light flaxen underdress.

"You like her?" Rorik said in-between gnawing meat off a boar thigh bone.

"Já." Denial was futile when his twin could feel his heart race whenever he looked at Edda—his new wife was a forbidden treat he ached to taste.

"Yet she does not please you?"

Ivvár sighed. So Rorik had felt his confusion too. He did not know how to answer. Despite the painful aching in his loins, he was not displeased with his wife. He found her unusual in a way that he could not put into words.

Edda turned, the light catching the white layer of clay and powder that coated her cheeks.

Everything about her was captivating. She made every day interesting and unpredictable. An image of her flashed in his mind from earlier in the evening as they had dressed for the feast.

She sat in front of her square of glass, using blue paint made from the woad leaves to paint little flicked wings from the corners of her eyes.

His breeches suddenly seemed too tight. Rapt, he watched her smear a touch of crushed raspberries to her cheeks and lips to finish.

"What?" she asked when she turned to face him.

She stole his breath.

The dark kohl line beneath the eye, white powder, and blue lines made her emerald eyes look like shimmering gems. Far from detracting from her beauty, the clay mask gave her the look of a goddess.

Yet, she did not respond to flattery. And that only made him want her more.

"Brother, does she vex you so you cannot speak?" Rorik had stopped eating and was looking at him oddly.

"Nei. Edda is a good woman. Samara and the other women are taken with her. Though we arrived a few days ago, many have come to the cottage seeking her healing."

"Then there is no trouble?"

Trouble? Nei. There was no trouble, rather a niggling unease that he could not shake. Seeing Edda easily fitting into clan life, teasing his brothers, and befriending their wives brought back many fond memories of being at home, of his childhood. Memories that should not have bothered him, yet they did.

He glanced at his brother. "Do you not miss Gottland when we are away?"

Rorik shook his head, his gaze puzzled.

"Coming home gets harder every time," Ivvár mused. He was so often away raiding and battling with Rorik that he'd forgotten how comforting it was to not be constantly on the move, to be surrounded by familiar faces, and to have time to breathe.

"Then do not leave," Rorik said, his tone sharp, challenging.

Ivvár looked at his twin pointedly. "You know why I follow you to battle."

Rorik huffed, glowering into his ale before downing it and slamming his mug on the table.

"I am glad that Edda has settled in well," Ivvár said, ignoring his twin's mood. And he *was* glad that Edda was confident in her role being völva to his clan. "Valen is glad to welcome a priestess to the island now that Samara is with child again."

"Yet?" Rorik grunted, making no effort to hide his irritation at being forced to speak more than was necessary.

Ivvár ran a hand through his hair, brushing it out of his eyes. "Edda behaves differently with me than everyone else." He motioned to where she stood with a broad smile, laughing at Valen throwing his young son up in the air. "With others, she is happy, yet she avoids me and cares naught for what I think. She will not even remove that paint and let me see her face."

His wife's affront bothered him more than he liked to admit. It reminded him far too much of the sting of Rorik's rejection.

Rorik smirked. "*You* wed to a woman that does not fall at your feet—the gods must be laughing."

"Not for long. I have resolved to win her over."

Rorik rose to his feet, his chair scraping against the floor. "One must fight hardest for the rarest treasures, Ivvár. Beware not to anger her lest she curse your manhood."

"Gods, do not even jest it. I have her vow not to curse me." Ivvár stilled as his brother's hand settled on his shoulder. He could not recall the last time Rorik had touched him.

Fingers dug into his shoulder. *You know what to do.* The words echoed in his mind as crisp as morning frost underfoot.

Ivvár watched as his twin crossed to the doorway and disappeared outside. Now Rorik would retreat to his hut tucked away in the forest, a full day's ride from Visby, alone but for the herds under his care.

Selfish!

His chest hurt at the thought of the weeks, or mayhap months, that would pass before Rorik would return to town. How could his twin walk away with such ease when for him, every day that they were apart, he could feel their connection die a little more?

Ivvár rose to his feet. No longer would he allow those closest to him to push him away—it was time to win over his wife.

"Valen," Ivvár said in greeting as he draped an arm over Edda's shoulder.

Her body stiffened at his touch, but she did not push him away or protest.

Valen nodded at him in greeting. "Brother."

"Samara, the feast is much improved since you married my brother. Mayhap you can fix his mead in time too," he teased, heartened by the smile that touched her lips. He had missed Samara, his brothers, and his clan.

Samara chuckled.

Valen feigned anger. "The mead will be much improved by the garden giving more herbs, Brother. And more vegetables would be welcomed too."

At his brother's words, Ivvár's light mood disappeared. He'd known that returning home would mean righting his mentor's neglected garden—everyone would expect it—it was why he had been so eager to raid this summer. His chest tightened at the thought of facing the place that Lasse had loved. He could not do it, not yet. Besides, he had a wife to woo.

"Wife, I find myself in want of your company." Ivvár let his fingers gently caress her shoulder, the slow sensual touch and her breathy gasp making him hard.

Edda brushed his hand aside like an ox swatting a fly. "Yet I do not."

Ivvár bent to whisper in her ear. "Liar." Wrapping an arm around her waist, he pulled her closer. She was as skittish as a cat when he was near, so the first step would be to get her used to his touch.

Samara's hand rose to cover the smile twitching her lips. He wondered what she was thinking. His brother's wife knew he had a honeyed tongue with the women, yet this was the first she had seen of him courting his wife.

Edda stiffened as he pressed her to his side.

Ivvár relaxed his hold, not wanting her to feel restrained. Feigning an affectionate nuzzling against her hair, he whispered in her ear. "Be calm, wife. I would hold you in my arms."

Her head whipped around, her eyes wide, panicked. She leaned away but stopped before pulling out of his embrace, realizing they had an audience.

Samara's brow furrowed in confusion.

His heart sank, his arms falling limp at his sides. Noticing a pounding heart or the lip-biting of wavering reluctance was as familiar to him as the silent hum of swinging a sword. But Edda was not reluctant—she had been rigid in his arms, tremoring.

She fears me.

Everything he thought he knew of her shattered, and he saw the truth—Edda had borne suffering that left scars on her mind. Rage heated his blood. Who had hurt his wife?

Valen turned to stare at him, puzzled, as Edda shuffled further away.

His face burned hot at his brother's questioning gaze. He knew that Valen was wondering if he had hurt her, had forced himself on his new bride, mayhap, even if his years of raiding had left him with the same dark appetites as Rorik. He stared back, unwavering. He would not be shamed for something he did not do.

Valen wrapped his arms around Samara, pulling her back against his side to step away, tactfully allowing Ivvár a moment of privacy with his wife.

"Keep your hands to yourself," Edda whispered so only he could hear.

"But they feel so good on you, and we are husband and wife." His tone was playful, but he made no move to pull her back into his arms. He would not touch her, not when she was unwilling.

"I am not like other wives," she shot back.

"Nei. You certainly are not," he replied, looking at her pointedly. Sweet words and shallow ploys would not work on Edda, and he could not help but admire her more for it.

Her jaw hardened, defiance lighting her eyes as she waved a hand at him dismissively. "Do not throw stones, Ivvár, for you have neglected your duties for years."

"What?"

Edda lifted the cup in her hands, her eyes locked on his as she sipped daintily. "You would do well to concentrate less on me and more on your duties. You are supposed to tend to the garden, are you not? Have the beds been prepared for the spring sowing?"

He knew her game, having used it often himself. She was lashing out to hide her fear, to reassert her strength. Still, her words had him struggling against the shame of allowing his mentor's legacy to fall to ruin out of loyalty to a brother who offered none in return. *Unworthy.* He could see the accusation in her eyes, felt it in his heart, and knew it to be true.

"What did you say?" To whom had she been speaking?

Edda smiled at him sweetly. To others, it would look like the smile of a woman enamored with her new husband, but he knew better. "Samara told me that the village garden is your responsibility. Yet you have been so busy raiding and whoring that you have neglected it."

He clenched his teeth until the sudden flare of his temper ebbed. "I oversee the kitchen gardens." He did not tell her that his father had foisted his role in the gardens on him, just as he had the trades of all the Eriksson brothers. At least he had enjoyed it for a time.

The tinkling timbre of Edda's laugh floated upward and

outward around the room, the feigned mirth of one well-practiced at courtly deception. "The women tend the kitchen garden. Even so, the meager harvest means Samara must trade for more produce. And don't tell me you work in the fields or the Jarl's orchard. I have seen the men toiling there day after day without you."

She went too far! Yet he refused to react and let her claim the win. Adept as she was at courtly antics and throwing barbed insults, he was better, much better. None could bend another to their will with more skill than he nor match his talent at feigning pleasantness while maneuvering for an advantage.

"What does it matter to you, Edda?"

Edda shook her head and shot him a pitying look. "It matters to all. The village garden could feed and heal many, but not in the overgrown mess it is now."

Bile rose in his throat.

"Talk not of my wifely duties when you so obviously neglect yours. Only a wastrel would rather fight and rut…" she said in a sweet tone that felt like a blade finding its mark. "…than honor his duty to feed his people."

Shame silenced his tongue. He could not fault her reasoning. His drinking and wild behavior had begun as an excuse to avoid the garden and then quickly became a habit. Lasse's disappointed frown at his half-hearted efforts in the garden before he slunk off to drink until dawn had only made it worse.

Only fools cast their gift aside.

Lasse's words had fallen on deaf ears. His mentor had never understood that he was torn between joy and loyalty— the pleasure he felt with his hands in his dirt, nurturing life from the earth, and his devotion to his twin, who loathed his days working with the shepherd.

He'd been forced to choose.

Unable to be happy whilst Rorik was miserable, he'd avoided the garden, marriageable women, anything that would bring joy. And in a pathetic rebellion of self-pity at the unfairness of his life, he'd fought, drank, and rutted. And then Lasse had died, and he'd continued to drown himself in ale, sorrow, and regret. The last insult that Lasse had hurled at him was true—he was a stubborn fool.

"Come, Edda. You must try a peach," Samara said, breaking the uncomfortable silence.

Ivvár watched as the women disappeared into the crowd. Lasse had entrusted him with the care of the garden, yet he shamed his friend with its neglect. He turned to face his brother, the Jarl he had failed. "I planned to speak to you of the garden. I—"

Valen pinned him with a concerned stare. "I know it is hard for you."

"I will replant in time for an autumn harvest. I promise." Regret that he had chosen a path that would take him yet further from his twin hit like a fist to the chest, but he pushed it aside.

"You will stay and care for Lasse's garden?" Valen looked at him with a combination of both surprise and skepticism.

"Já. Lasse deserves better from me."

Valen studied him thoughtfully. "You deserve better too, brother."

Ivvár shrugged. "Mayhap. I have lived the wastrel life for many years, yet it brings me no joy."

"You cannot save him, Ivvár. It is time to let Rorik find his way. You need this new beginning with Edda. You deserve a happy life."

Ivvár considered his brother's words. Mayhap it was time he stopped mourning, or began mourning. Whichever it was that would get him back to his old self. If Rorik wanted to be lonely and miserable, then so be it.

"Ivvár?"

Straightening his shoulders, Ivvár nodded at Valen. He needed to act like a warrior, not a whelp, and move through the pain of losing his friend.

Valen slapped him on the back and thrust a cup of ale into his hands. "Tending to the garden that has fed the clan for generations is a good place to begin, Ivvár. The addition to our winter stores will be appreciated. Now tell me, what strife is there with your new bride?"

Ivvár ran a hand through his hair and then shook his head. "It is naught. A lover's quarrel."

Valen studied him for a moment, then nodded in sympathy.

Ivvár searched the room until he found Edda sitting at a table surrounded by women. "She is a challenge to be sure."

"Does there exist a woman that is not?"

Ivvár chuckled. "Marriage is not what I expected— strangers living separate lives."

Valen raised an eyebrow. "It is only so, if that is what you wish."

Ivvár looked down at the cup of golden liquid. "It is not." He set his cup down on the table beside where they stood, the allure of drinking to avoid his problems gone.

Valen nodded in understanding. "A true marriage is built stone by stone, brother. Your wife is as skittish as a new foal. You must tread slowly, with kindness and a gentle hand. Talk to her. Discover who she is and what she desires, then give it to her."

Ivvár nodded. "I will heed your counsel." What did his wife desire? Hollow seduction would never win Edda over—

he could see that now. He needed to discover the woman behind the mask and gain her favor.

"I will show Edda we can build a good life together." As he rebuilt the garden by pulling the weeds and clearing away the overgrowth, he would treat his marriage with the same tender care.

And he would not cease until he had won her heart.

CHAPTER EIGHT

EDDA

*T*he sun had barely passed its zenith in the sky when the squeak of the door opening echoed through the small cottage.

Why is he home? Edda's fingers tightened around the runestick. After their heated words at the feast, they'd spent cold nights side by side before Ivvár departed to work in the garden at dawn.

Ivvár stood at the doorway, stomping mud off his boots.

Ignoring him, she continued to carve with the small dagger. Her blade rendered the runes of Ingwaz, Uruz, Jera, and Fehu to aid the growth and potency of the healing plants in her garden. Wood shavings fell like snowflakes, each careful pass of the blade imbuing magic into the carving.

"What in Helheim?"

Startled, Edda glanced over her shoulder.

Ivvár had stopped short at the sight of the chaos of their home. Exhaustion and surprise marred his handsome features, along with a smear of mud across one cheek.

Edda turned back to her carving. He was mistaken if he thought three days of hard toil on a task that had long been his duty would win him any favor. As she worked, her gaze drifted over the counter—it was a mess of freshly cut herbs tied into small bundles ready to dry, along with a large clump of dirt-covered ginger roots. Strewn haphazardly amongst the foliage was an assortment of small glass bottles that her father had gifted her from his travels to the east. Slowly, this was beginning to feel like her home.

"Edda?"

Sighing heavily, she turned to face Ivvár. Best be done with pleasantries that cannot be avoided when sharing a house. Her skin prickled as he gawked at the muddy orange circles around her eyes and the charcoal-black nose that gave her the likeness of a red fox. Each day his stares became longer, more thorough, as though he was trying to unravel the secrets she hid beneath the paint.

"Ivvár," she replied, placing a dagger on the counter.

His blue eyes met hers. "What are you doing?"

"Carving a rune-stick for the garden."

"I left early and did not break my fast." The pulsing vein in his jaw signaled that she was trying his patience.

"What of it?"

Ivvár ran his hand through his hair the way he did when he was frustrated—often of late. "I wish to eat a meal cooked by my wife."

"Wish away, husband. It is more likely that the sun will shine in mid-winter." Edda picked up the dagger and crossed to the door, pausing to look over her shoulder as she spoke. "You prepare your food, and I shall sow the garden."

Rocking back on his heels, Ivvár nodded. His lips twitched in amusement. "Bread and cheese then."

Edda walked around the cottage toward the small plot. Her garden. Ivvár would not ruin this vital ritual. She had long wanted a place to grow and nurture the plants she needed for healing and magic. She adored this garden with well-organized beds sheltered from the wind by a ramshackle wooden fence. Someone had once nurtured this small plot— she could feel it in the soil—and now she would too.

Using the dagger, she pricked her finger and rubbed the blood on the rune-stick. Fingers tight on the carved wood, she closed her eyes and began to chant, calling on the gods and sending her magic outward over the land she claimed.

A low hum sounded in her ears. *What is that?* Her eyes snapped open, searching for the unfamiliar vibration.

Air shifted as Ivvár came to a stop behind her. "I have decided that I will prepare the meal for us both," he whispered in her ear before stepping back.

The nape of her neck warmed, and Edda knew he would be staring at her if she turned.

Ignore him.

Gathering her thoughts, Edda crouched to thrust the rune-stick into the soft earth. The embrace of the land flowed through her body in a crashing wave of pleasure that she felt in the gentle sunlight warming her skin and a sudden rush of coolness in the earth beneath her feet. Not wanting to let her guard down around Ivvár, she held back the contented sigh that threatened to escape. Plants grown here would be imbued with powerful magic to help her heal and commune with the gods. Gathering her skirts, she wove through the overgrown beds to get to work.

"You like my garden?" Ivvár leaned against the cottage wall with one ankle crossed over the other, watching her.

"It is *my* garden now." Lowering herself to her knees, she

began to pull weeds and place them in a pile on the narrow path

"Já. What is mine is yours, little wife."

Placing her hands on her hips, she glared at him. "Mayhap you could give me your silence then?"

His laugh was deep and warm. "What will you plant?" he asked, his hands whittling away at a piece of wood as he watched her work.

"Rosemary."

"It is good for aching heads and sore muscles. Likely you have much need for it in your tinctures."

Though aware he had spent time in gardens, it surprised her that he knew of the plant's healing properties. It was unusual that his father, having no tolerance for idleness in his children, had ensured that his sons learned a trade.

Turning her head to look at him, Edda raised an eyebrow, intent on driving him from her sanctuary. "I would not need to plant rosemary here if it were grown in the communal garden as it should be."

"Apologies. I shall sow some in the morn. Angelica too."

Naught. Not the slightest glimmer that her blow affected him. Huffing, she dug her hands back into the earth, turning the soil over.

"Are there other plants you need?"

"A healer needs many plants." Edda let the cool earth fall through her fingers, the rough play of the soil on her skin a soothing balm to her angry mood.

"I know you loathe me, but I'm trying, Edda."

A twinge of guilt gnawed at her. Since she had confronted him, Ivvár *had* been working in the garden. Each morn, Samara delighted in telling her the number of carts of debris hauled away the day before.

Her hands stilled in the dirt, her eyes lifting. "I do not loathe you."

Ivvár still leaned against the wall, but the wood carving had disappeared from his hands, his fingers now using the dagger to remove the dirt beneath his fingernails. Even relaxed, he exuded power, strength, and purpose.

His blue gaze met hers, darkened, grew wild.

Edda looked away to shield her eyes. Stretching out, she placed another daisy atop the small pile she had set aside in honor of the goddess Freya.

"Edda…"

From the corner of her eye, she glimpsed Ivvár pushing off the wall, his long fingers moving swiftly to slide his dagger into the sheath at his belt.

"The angelica would grow well over there in the sun," he said, his powerful legs moving in long strides until he stopped in front of her.

She looked up at his angular jaw and kind eyes.

"May I bring you some for planting?"

Edda tore her gaze away, only to be confronted with the sight of the fabric of his pants pulled tight across his muscular thighs and the bulging evidence of sizable manhood directly in front of her face. Her breath caught, but she refused to lower her eyes. This was no mistake. Ivvár was teasing her, seducing her, and he would never leave if he thought there was any hope that she would succumb to his wiles.

"What are you doing, Ivvár?" She returned her gaze to his, confident that he would not see beyond the defiant jut of her chin and her brave stare to the riotous chaos she felt inside when he was this close.

"What am I doing?"

"Surely you can see that I do not want you in *my* garden."

Her heart raced as his eyes raked over her body. Straightening her back, she bore his perusal in silence, hoping he would not find what he sought.

"I thought mayhap we could tend *our* garden together." A devastating grin accompanied his words.

Our garden? She swallowed hard as his words rendered her speechless. She knew there were no plants in the garden to which he referred.

An image flashed in her mind of Ivvár shirtless, sweat dripping down his muscular chest as he turned soil with his shovel, and then became flickering firelight on a bed covered in soft furs. Her lower lip trembled as she struggled to find her voice. Annoyance and an uncomfortable yearning coursed through her veins.

"Edda?" Ivvár pressed.

Pulling furiously on a stuck root, she showered herself in dirt before tossing it on the now sizable pile of debris. "Do you not have your garden to tend?"

"You seem very interested in my garden, Edda. I hope you will join me there."

Panic had words tumbling from her mouth. "I shall *not!*"

Ivvár's brow crinkled as he chuckled and tossed her a cheeky wink and boyish smile that would have made a lesser woman melt.

Not her. She was as icy as the tundra of the northlands, on the outside at least.

"Are you never serious, Ivvár? You must fix that overgrown mess. If pests get into the kitchen garden or there is one bad harvest, there will not be enough food for the clan. Your people will starve."

Ivvár smiled at her softly and walked around her, seemingly unfazed by her accusation. "Gratitude for your care for my clan. The garden will be planted after Olaf hauls a dung cart from his farm at dawn."

Relieved that she had distracted him, Edda waved a hand dismissively. "Very good. Now leave me be."

Ivvár knelt on one knee behind her, his body wrapping around hers until their bodies touched.

Her stomach fluttered traitorously. She could feel him, all of him. The solid press of his chest against her back, his strong arms surrounding her, and the rigid length of his manhood against her buttocks.

"As you wish."

The heat of his breath on her earlobe made her shiver.

"Although I am loathe to leave the sight of my little wife with her hands in the earth and the sunlight shimmering in her hair."

As he reached forward, her lips parted in surprise, his solidness pressing in on her, sheltering her. Her skin prickled with awareness. His scent was a delicious combination of earth and fresh-cut wood.

Slowly, his long fingers covered hers, his gentle touch moving their hands downward.

Edda lowered her gaze, watching as their joined hands pressed the wooden stake he'd carved into the dirt. This honoring and making an offering to the earth that surrounded their home felt like more than a ritual. Ivvár had carved the uruz rune into the sapling to promote growth. It felt like a promise—a promise to honor their home, their marriage, and her.

Releasing her fingers, Ivvár gently brushed stray hairs off her face. His eyes captured hers as she turned to look back at him.

Her heartbeat sounded like rolling thunder in her ears.

He ran his fingertips down her curls, teasing the strands in the sunlight. "Beautiful," he whispered, soft, reverential.

Her hands shook, her chest aching as she forgot to breathe.

"I have a gift for mastering neglected gardens…" he said, his voice deep, sensual. "And I am especially fond of fiery autumn ones." After speaking the words so softly she thought she had misheard, Ivvár rose to his feet and strolled away.

CHAPTER NINE

IVVÀR

*a*fter unfastening his trousers, Ivvàr pushed them down over his hips and slung them across the chair. At this point, he would usually pull on his sleeping pants, but they had shared a bed for a full moon now, and he would hide naught this eve. He could feel Edda watching him. He'd caught her peeking a few nights ago when he disrobed for bed. He'd seen the flush as red as a wild strawberry creep up her neck, even beneath the mask.

Delicious!

"What are you doing?" Edda asked with a shakiness to her voice that he had not heard before.

Lifting his chin, he strengthened his resolve. He could not waver, or she would never see him as her husband. "I mean you no harm. I prefer to sleep naked." He kept his back to her, knowing that if he turned, she would close her eyes and pretend that she'd not been admiring his buttocks.

"I would have you clothed in our bed."

"And I would not," he replied honestly. The first step to making this a marriage in truth would be for Edda to become accustomed to seeing his naked body. Lifting his arms over his head, he stretched and flexed.

"Why do you stretch?"

Ivvár smiled. So, she *was* looking. "I ache from pulling weeds and turning earth." He could not tell her that he wanted her gaze to linger on him longer, nor that he wanted the sight of him to heat her blood just as she did his. It may be many moons before Edda would not flinch when he slid into the bed beside her naked. And longer still before she welcomed him into her body. He could wait. He was a patient man. Turning slowly, he looked at his wife.

Edda lay on her back with her head turned away from him, her auburn curls secured atop her head with a leather tie, exposing her neck.

Gods, those curls! He wanted to breathe them in and run his hands through them as he kissed her. With each sunrise, he thanked the gods that she did not try to tame her hair into a long braid like the other women of the clan. The merest glimpse of those wild red curls made his manhood painfully hard, a state he often needed to attend to in the bathhouse.

"Edda?" He hoped that she would be brave enough to look upon him naked. He wanted to feel the heat of her gaze, see a flicker of admiration or desire that signaled that she felt something, anything, for him.

She turned, her lashes lifting slowly.

His heart raced.

Her face was painted in the sleek, elegant features of a cat, with the very tip of her nose darkened with kohl and dainty whiskers crossing her cheeks.

Son of Óðinn! Ivvár swallowed hard, forcing down the groan that rumbled in his chest. He was hard as steel. He'd wanted her to become accustomed to the sight of his manhood, but not standing upright like this, engorged and leaking at the tip.

Her eyes widened, and she looked away. "Ivvár! Make it go down."

"I cannot." He turned away hastily. By the gods, that was even worse! The tapestry he'd removed for beating had not been replaced, and now the hearth fire behind him was casting an overly elongated shadow of his rigid cock on the wall.

Her breathy gasp was almost a whimper.

Thor's hammer! He'd not intended to terrify her.

"It is big, but you will soon be glad for it."

"I will *not!*" The blankets rustled as she rolled over.

Ivvár smiled at her vehement denial. At least she was not screaming or running. He placed the lantern beside the bed and slid beneath the covers. Wrapping an arm around her waist, he tugged her closer.

"What are you doing?" she hissed, her body tense, frozen.

"It is cold this eve. We will keep each other warm." The softness of her curves against his hard warrior body had him yearning to remove the thin nightdress that separated them, but he would not.

"Nightclothes will keep you warm, Ivvár." Edda squirmed to get away, cursing under her breath when he did not move.

"Sleep now, wife." Loosening his grip on her, he lay still, waiting for her to protest.

Silence. She did not move.

Her soft rosemary scent surrounded him as though he were lying in a spring meadow. Motionless, he focused on the gentle rhythm of his breath, savoring the moment. Edda was letting him in, allowing him to hold her, and he would do naught to risk losing her trust.

Slowly her muscles loosened, and she sank into the bed, calm and restful in his arms.

Ivvár's eyes drifted closed, the tension easing from his body. All the waiting was worthwhile for this sweet reward, this fragile trust she had gifted him.

Shuffling closer still, he exhaled a heavy breath against her neck. Now that he knew he had won her trust, he could woo her.

Edda exhaled, her head rolling back in a silent plea. Her body did not lie—she wanted him.

Encouraged, Ivvár feathered a light kiss on the sensitive curve between her neck and shoulder. He swallowed hard to keep from groaning. Her taste was as sweet as honeyed nectar.

Edda whimpered and pressed back further into his embrace.

Her innocence was enchanting, made him want to take her, claim her, show her the pleasures of the flesh. He needed to be her first, her last, her only. Ivvár pressed his lips to her throat and trailed soft kisses upward, her skin smooth and sweet on his lips.

More. He needed more. He nipped at the tender flesh of her earlobe.

"Já." He groaned into her hair when she shifted, her behind brushing against his manhood. He knew what she wanted, what she needed. His mouth found the hollow of her neck, emboldened when she did not object. "Did you know the scent of a woman is stronger here?"

A moment later, Edda was across the bed and scowling at him. "Do not seek to seduce me."

Ivvár rested his head on his hand and looked at her. Even angry, she was beautiful. "I want to show you what can be between man and wife."

"This cannot happen. I told you there would be no bedding, ever."

Ivvár smiled indulgently and shuffled closer. Her fervor told him she *had* thought of bedding him, that mayhap she was afraid to let him close for fear of succumbing to her desires. He leaned down, his mouth hovering above hers, breathing in the sweet taste of the air as she exhaled.

Her breath caught, confirming his suspicion. "Ivvár…"

Dipping his head, Ivvár ran his tongue over the fullness of her lips. Exploring, testing, giving her time to deny him.

Her lips parted, soft and irresistible.

Já. It was the acquiescence he had been awaiting. His mouth covered hers hungrily, his tongue dipping inside in the slow sensual rhythm of a lover intent on savoring pleasure.

Edda moaned softly, her arms wrapping around his neck.

Ivvár fought to restrain his desire to devour her, her every shiver and throaty moan fanning the raging wildfire coursing through his veins. Time slowed to a crawl as he kept the kiss languid and gentle.

Rosemary and honey.

He was adrift. Her taste was intoxicating. The long weeks of gaining her trust made her ardent response all the sweeter.

"I want you. All of you," he said and then took her mouth, once more succumbing to the rising tide of their fervor.

Not yet! The words echoed like a warning horn in his mind. He could not bed her when she was still withholding so much of herself. Not now, not like this. He wanted *all* of her when they made love. He pulled back, bereft at the sudden loss of her lips.

"Nei," Edda protested, her hand pulling him downward at the back of his neck.

Ivvár dipped his head to press a gentle kiss to the top of her head and then pulled back.

Edda rolled over, her body filling the space between them, seeking his own. Her eyes drifted open, heavy-lidded and clouded with desire. Her lips parted, but she did not speak—she just looked at him.

Never had he seen a woman more beautiful than his wife, dazed and panting from being kissed senseless, with those sweet little whiskers on her cheeks. He brushed a finger down over the curve of her cheek. "I love the cat," he said softly. "Do you want to play, kitten?"

Her brow furrowed in confusion.

"Where is your tail?" He pressed his fingers to the curve at the base of her spine, the hard bone he knew to be more sensitive to touch than even her most tender places.

Edda brought a hand up to stifle her laugh.

He grinned down at her. "Do not hide it. I love to hear you laugh."

Their eyes locked. The air between them thickened, bonding them.

He gently brushed a stray curl from her face and tucked it behind her ear. At last, he felt close to his wife, truly connected. He wanted to burrow himself inside her, to know those deepest parts of her that she hid from the world.

"Take off the paint, Edda. I want to see you."

The air chilled, the severing of their connection instant. Brutal.

Wrenching herself from his embrace, Edda shuffled to the farthest side of the bed, her eyes wide.

Silently, he cursed his foolishness. He had pushed too hard. Lost her.

CHAPTER TEN

EDDA

*W*ith her heart thundering like a herd of wild horses on the run, Edda dug her fingernails into her palms.

Breathe.

Inhaling a gulping breath, she focused on the stinging bite of her broken flesh. The haze of passion slowly faded, leaving only the tender ache of her swollen lips. Eventually, she lifted her head and studied those blue eyes. They both knew something had changed, had shifted with that kiss. All her defenses had crumbled with his gentle teasing lips, unlocking a passion within her that could not be undone. Her surrender had been wild, reckless. Absolute.

The slight curving of his lips confirmed he knew it too. "It is time, Edda. Take off the mask, and let me see you."

Her magic recoiled. His every word felt like a blade slashing through the hazy remnants of her desire. Each painful cut destroyed her.

"Mayhap the cat wants to come out to play?"

His teasing jibe fell on deaf ears. Her lungs seized—reality slamming into her with brutal force. The cat mask had lured Ivvár into seducing her, the very thing which shielded her true self from him. Ivvár did not want *her*. He wanted the woman in the cat mask. As soon as he saw the plain Edda, her bared unsightly face, he would realize his error.

Hideous Edda!

She would repulse him—she knew it as surely as she knew the sun would set and the moon would rise.

"I cannot." Her whisper was hoarse, pained. Cold fear coiled around her heart and squeezed. *Never.* She could never wipe off the mask, for she could not bear to see his disgust when he saw all she was not. Not beautiful, not even comely, just plain with no redeeming features.

She sucked in a breath and closed her eyes. The last time she'd seen that look, as Ubbe had laughed and called her the hideous sister, her heart had shattered into jagged pieces that left her as broken and ugly within as she was on the outside. Mayhap it would be wiser to show Ivvár her face—no man wanted to share his seed with an unappealing woman.

Nei. She could not do it.

Even if she were brave enough to remove the layers of clay and paint, a simple act that would surely end Ivvár's game of seduction, the thought of giving up the mask that was her armor, of being vulnerable before this man, any man, had her entire being recoiling in protest. With her mask came power and respect, and she would not give that away for anything.

"I cannot have you see me," she whispered.

"You can, Edda. Trust me."

Edda could hear the disappointment in his voice. It was for the best that she stopped this now, before he realized that she was damaged and sought the arms of another. Forcing her eyes open, she looked up into his face.

"We should not have kissed. It was a mistake." She didn't even bother to pretend that she had not come dangerously close to giving herself to him, to surrendering her body and with it, her völva magic.

Ivvár's gaze was kind as his hand settled on her shoulder, his touch burning her skin where her nightdress had fallen away.

"Do. Not. Touch. Me." She shrugged him off and pulled the blankets up to her chin. Her senses reeled—his touch was a weakness she could not afford.

"Edda—" Ivvár sounded hurt, wounded at her rebuff.

"There will be no more kissing," she interrupted him. "No more touching."

His brow furrowed. "Why? I know you liked it. What are you afraid of?"

Her mind raced. What answer would placate him without revealing the truth? She'd told herself it was to retain her magic, but her fear went deeper. She *had* liked it, and she was not fool enough to think that denial would convince him otherwise. Her fears were more than she could give voice to — stripping away all else and facing the stranger beneath the mask, Ivvár seeing her bared face and then casting her aside, being vulnerable.

"Is it more than your magic that you are afraid to lose?"

A hollow ache filled her chest as the harsh truth cut through the barricades around her heart. All she had lost came rushing back—her hopes for a family, birthing, and nurturing a child. Desperate, she had buried those slivers of hope in the darkest corners of her heart. They were dreams that belonged to the lithe and beautiful that walked amongst them, not the broken who were fated to walk alone. Not her, never her.

"Edda, tell me." His blue eyes were fixed on her, determined, possessive.

"It matters not. What is lost is gone."

"What did you lose?"

"Childish dreams are long dead."

"If you tell me your hopes—"

"So you can what, Ivvár? Trample on them like…" *Gods!* She had nearly revealed too much. She needed him to understand that he could not fix these problems between them, that their marriage, as it was now, was all it would ever be. "What I want is to be völva. For that to be, you must accept that we will not lie together."

His expression darkened. His steady look left no doubt that he had noticed her mistake. He knew someone had hurt her. "Denying your desires will only make them burn hotter. Trust me—I know well that they will never go away."

"Let it go, Ivvár."

He pinned her with a solemn stare. "I shall never give up on you or this marriage. You do not know me well yet, but you shall soon."

The gentle tone of his voice brought tears to her eyes. Turning away, she muttered a curse. She did not want his kindness, not when it made it harder to loathe him. Tamping down her emotion, she met his gaze and spoke with unwavering resolve. "This marriage is an alliance between our families, that is all. You agreed to give up your husbandly rights."

Ivvár gave her a slow, boyish smile. Amusement lit his eyes. "Not all of them, Edda."

"W-what?"

"There are other ways to give pleasure than claiming a woman's body, and I mean to show you *all* of them."

Her heart lurched, and her fingers tightened on the

woolen blanket. Her skin ached for his touch. She bit down on her lip, angry that her body would betray her. How was she to resist this man over many years of marriage?

Ivvár's lips twitched as though he were holding back a grin. The fool thought he had bested her.

Her temper flared at his overconfidence. He was mistaken if he thought using wordplay to bend the rules would make her cede. Nei. It merely firmed her resolve to withstand his attentions. And he thought he could convince her to share her body by giving pleasure rather than taking—What did that even mean? The very act itself was a taking of a woman's body. Wasn't it?

Ivvár winked, seemingly unperturbed by the glare she was leveling at him. Sighing contentedly, he rolled over and shuffled backward until the warmth of his back rested against her side. "Goodnight, little cat wife. Sleep well."

She did not.

CHAPTER ELEVEN

IVVÁR

*I*vvár turned the earth with a spade, moving in the fluid motion he'd thought long forgotten. He relished the crunch of soil and the familiar stretch and ache of long-unused muscles. With each passing day, the feeling of being embraced by Lasse's walled garden deepened and settled with the same comforting familiarity as a warm fire on a winter night.

Bees hummed, timid green shoots unfurled and stretched toward the sun, and the sweet scent of spring blossoms lingered on the breeze. It was as if Gerda, goddess of gardens, was reminding him he belonged here, tending the earth. Ivvár sucked a deep breath and leaned on the wooden handle. A warm glow filled him as he looked across at the three beds he had cleared and turned since dawn.

Leaves rustled on the highest branch of the oldest apple tree.

"Come out of there," he said to the gangly dark-haired youth perched on a gnarled weathered branch.

The boy glared down at him.

"I am Ivvár. What is your name?" He'd realized that he had company this morn when he'd arrived to find his tools lined up neatly against the old wooden shed with the dirt wiped from them. All day he had worked while ignoring the interloper so as not to scare him away. On his own very first day in the garden, Lasse had set him to tending the tools— that this boy had done the same felt like an omen that it was time to ensure that all Lasse had taught him would be passed on, that there would be another to care for this place after he was gone too.

"I am Kal." The wiry youth leaped to the ground and brushed his hands off on pants smeared with dirt.

Ivvár motioned him over, but the boy ignored his summons.

Turning on his heel, Kal walked to the bed of cabbage seedlings. Bending, he tore the plants from the dirt and tossed them aside.

Thor's hammer! Ivvár crossed to him in three strides, his hand closing over the boy's wrist to halt the destruction. "Stop! You are destroying them." Loosening his grip, Ivvár looked down at the boy. "What is wrong?"

Tears welled in the boy's eyes.

"What is it?"

Hands clenched into fists at his sides, Kal's chest heaved as tears streamed down his cheeks. The boy was young, mayhap no more than ten summers. Too young to be filled with this much wrath and turmoil. His anger reminded Ivvár of Rorik—wounded, pained, raw.

"Tell me, Kal."

Kal shook his head and looked away.

Ivvár suspected he knew the answer. Kal was the son of Baldr, a warrior who had drowned himself in ale since he had returned wounded from the raids last summer. No doubt this was the cause of the boy's angst.

Kal winced but remained silent, unwilling to speak ill of his father. The boy had an admirable sense of honor.

"Does he hurt you? Or your mother?" Ivvár thought not, but had to ask, for ale could bring out the worst in men.

"Nei!" Kal shook his head vehemently. "He would never."

Ivvár nodded, relieved that he had not been mistaken about the warrior that had fought at his side. "Is it the ale? You can tell me."

Kal looked away, ashamed.

He looked at the boy thoughtfully. All men coped with the ravages of war in their way, but most did better if they had a purpose. Baldr had only a small cottage on the outskirts of the village and no land of his own to farm. If he had not found work, his family must be surviving on the dwindling spoils of last summer's raids.

"How many summers do you have?"

"Eleven."

The boy looked strong, though mayhap a little thin. If much of Baldr's coin was going to ale, then likely the only food he was getting was the night meal served in the Great Hall. That was no way for a warrior who'd fought many battles for his clan, nor his family, to live. He would speak to Valen about finding Baldr work, a way for his clansman to provide for his family and keep his honor.

As Ivvár mused, Kal wiped his tears with the sleeve of his stained tunic and composed himself before lifting his gaze. When their eyes met, the boy did not cower or look away. His green eyes, though tinged with sadness, were determined and proud.

Já. This one has the heart of a warrior.

Ivvár placed a hand on his shoulder. "You cannot hurt the plants. Come," he said and then turned and walked away.

After a moment of hesitation, footsteps followed him across the grass.

"I will pay one dirham for each day you work with me in the garden." Retrieving the metal shovel, he held it out to the boy. "Will you work?" He would not repeat his father's mistake and force the boy into a livelihood. Kal must choose if he wanted to follow this path.

"Work?" Kal looked bewildered.

"Já. I was your age when I started tending the gardens. A boy of your years should be working and earning his keep. You enjoy being in the garden, já?"

Kal nodded, his dark hair flopping over his eyes. "My thanks for—"

Ivvár held up his hand, interrupting him. "Do not thank me so soon. You will work from dawn until the midday meal, and again until dusk. It will be hard at first, but you will learn much and may harvest from the garden to feed your kin."

Kal's eyes widened, and he nodded eagerly. "I...my thanks, Ivvár. I will not let you down."

"Good. Start digging. We have herbs to sow for my wife's healing plants."

~

Two beds filled with rosemary, angelica, and woad were sown when Kal eventually voiced his curiosity.

"Who taught you about the garden and plants?"

"Lasse Bjornsson. Like all my brothers, I was put to work in my tenth summer. I came here, to the garden."

"What happened to Lasse?"

"He died," Ivvár said, surprised that he could speak of the loss without losing his composure. Lasse's death had been a crushing blow that left him unable to return to the garden filled with so many memories, the hurt too deep to bear. Yet now, working alongside Kal to set the garden to rights felt as natural as the circle of seasons.

"Your brother that looks like you…"

"Já. Rorik."

Kal looked around, suddenly wary, as though expecting Rorik to jump out from behind a bush. "Did he work here too?"

Ivvár shook his head, a wry smile on his lips. "Nei. He was sent to tend the animals." He'd never told anyone that Rorik had crawled into his bed and sobbed uncontrollably about being forced to slaughter a lamb after his first day working with the shepherd. He had gone to his father and pleaded for Rorik to work in the garden with him, but the Jarl had been stubborn in his determination to separate them. Rorik had gone back to the shepherd and the slaughtering.

And neither of them was ever the same.

All pleasure at feeling earth on his hands, of watching a new shoot sprout to life, was quashed. Stolen. Ever loyal to his twin, he had decided not to allow himself that joy, not when Rorik suffered. And so, they had suffered together, yet apart.

"Why is he so bad-tempered? All of the children are afeared of him."

Ivvár lifted the water skin to his lips and drank. He would give anything to know the answer to that question. As the years had passed, he'd felt the cracks in his brother form, darkness seeping outward as the chasm between them grew.

Before long, the other half of him was unrecognizable, a stranger. The children were wise in their fear. Rorik reveled in the bloodlust of raiding with the ferocity of a man determined to hide from himself.

"He is troubled," Ivvár finally said, lacking a better explanation. He was weary of explaining and making excuses for his twin. For years he had tried to comfort Rorik, keeping the best vegetables for his brother and never speaking of the garden. Yet his twin had only retreated farther away with each passing day until he was beyond reach.

"Troubled like my father?"

"Já. Like your father."

"I want to help my Da."

"You are a dutiful son, but sometimes a man must find his own way out of the darkness." The truth of his words slammed into him—only Rorik could mend his brokenness. Too long he had spent devoted to an impossible task. It was time to move on, to focus on himself, the garden, and his marriage.

Kal looked at him, confused. "How will he find his way in the darkness?"

"Is your father a good man?" There was naught he could do for Rorik, but mayhap he could reunite this boy and his father.

"Já. His heart is true."

Reaching out, Ivvár ruffled the boy's hair affectionately. "Then mayhap he just needs to know that he is loved and to feel his son's embrace."

"Do you think?"

Ivvár shrugged. "My mother often said that her children were the light in her life."

Kal nodded thoughtfully. "Then I shall try it."

* * *

EDDA

Edda walked around her garden, ladling water onto her fledgling seedlings as she listened to the hum of bees dancing between the wildflowers at her ankles. Twitter of starlings wafted on the breeze as they flitted from branch to branch, searching for spring buds on the plum trees. The forest and the fields beyond the village were alive with fresh growth and abundance after the long fallow winter months.

Earth cooled the soles of her feet, grounding her. After the last winter frost had thawed and a thick covering of grass and flowers had covered the ground, she had kicked off her boots in favor of being barefoot.

"Well met, friend."

Edda watched Samara holding the hem of her deep blue gown aloft as she wove through the garden beds. She smiled at the waves of love she could feel emanating from the expectant mother for the child she carried.

"Well met, Samara." She smiled brightly at her new friend. "Are you feeling well now that your birthing time draws near?"

Soon the jarl's wife would be too busy caring for her new babe to have time to visit with her. She would miss this time they shared discussing healing, tinctures, and all Samara had learned from the healers in her homelands far to the east.

"You worry overmuch, Edda. The tea you made has helped to settle my stomach. I will be glad to have you with me when this babe is born."

Edda moved onto the next garden bed, knowing that Samara would follow. "It will be a blessing. I devoted my

days to guiding novices before I wed Ivvár. I thought it
would be many years before I attended another birthing."

"You did not attend the women in nearby villages?"
Samara shuffled past her and then turned back with her
hands resting on her swollen stomach. The babe would come
soon. Birthing often came early with the second child.

"We were called on afterward for blessings, but the village
women cared for their own for birthing."

Samara placed a hand on her shoulder and squeezed
gently. "Valen and I are relieved you will welcome this little
one."

Edda dipped her head respectfully. "You are too kind."
Whether it was Samara bringing her honey or Valen
ensuring she was included in those sent to forage in the
forest, she had received only kindness from them. Watching
the easy comradery and genuine affection between the
Eriksson brothers and their wives reminded her of all she
had lost—a father and a sister she'd once adored.

Samara's gaze swept around the garden plot. "You have
done much these last weeks. I can see this will be a
wonderful garden, Edda."

Pushing aside her melancholy, she forced a smile. "Já. It
will if I can keep Ivvár out."

A soft burst of laughter escaped Samara. "What has your
husband done now?"

Edda huffed loudly. At every turn, Ivvár was poking his
nose where it did not belong, taunting her with his interfering ways. "It is my garden. I ordered him to stay away, but
he sneaks in when I am gone."

"Is he hurting your plants?" Samara narrowed her eyes,
looking around for signs of destruction. "I would not think
him capable of such a thing."

Edda shook her head. "Nei. The plants grow well."

Samara cocked her head to one side, her long dark locks falling in gentle waves over and around her protruding stomach. "So, what ails you then? What does he do?"

"First, the piles of weeds I had dug out of the beds disappeared."

"Ah." Samara raised an eyebrow. "And what did you do?"

"I refuse to show him that his games bother me, so I did not mention it." And neither had Ivvár, but she'd noticed a bounce in his step that eve accompanied by a satisfied smirk he'd tried to hide.

"But it continued?"

Edda pursed her lips and nodded as she placed the pail and ladle on the ground. It had only worsened. "He turned all of those beds." She pointed to the far side of the garden where she had pushed the soil into neat rows and planted burdock and wormwood. "I know it was him—he used dried dung that he told me was being delivered to *his* garden."

Samara brought a hand up to stifle her chuckle. "How dare he!" she said in a mocking tone.

Hands on hips, Edda ignored her and continued. "Then, just yesterday, all of my tallest seedlings had been tied to fresh-cut stakes!"

Samara shook her head, now clearly amused. "Goodness! Whatever will you do with a husband that wants to help your garden grow?"

Edda blushed. "He…he is interfering."

A look of understanding dawned on Samara's face.

Edda squirmed. She had told Samara that bedding Ivvár would mean losing her powers. Yet still, she wanted none of her friend's pity.

Samara smiled—her expression far too joyful for this discussion. "He is wooing you, Edda."

"What?" *Wooing her?*

Samara gazed off into the distance, one finger tapping at her chin thoughtfully. "Clever man!" When she turned back, her eyes gleamed with newfound knowledge. "Ivvár knows that your plants are important to who you are and what you do as a healer."

"He does?"

Samara nodded. "He likes you, Edda. Caring for your garden is his way of showing you that he cares about your needs and will provide for you."

Ivvár cared for her? The thought was too confusing to fathom. "H-he has been here today. I can feel it," she stammered.

"Wonderful!" Samara clapped her hands together and then strode off. "Let us discover what he has done this time."

Edda clenched and released the fabric of her dress as she pondered the notion that her husband, or any man, might like her. *Surely not?*

"Oh!"

Samara's gasp pulled her from her musings. "What is it?"

"You must come and see."

Heart in her throat, Edda crossed to where Samara stood beside an overgrown mess of brambles. She didn't want to see, was afraid. Afraid that like that kiss, once seen, this deed to win her favor would weaken her defenses. Summoning her courage, she looked at where Samara pointed.

Nestled amongst the weeds and brambles, one lone plant topped with yellow star-shaped flowers reached for the sun.

"Is that…" Samara's awed whisper trailed off.

Edda swallowed hard. "Madder," she whispered, breathless. It was the flower of the rarest of all the dye plants.

Samara leaned down for a closer look. "The plant that makes the red dye used on the raven banner flown atop longships as they enter battle?"

"Já. It is made from the roots." Cloth dyed in the much-coveted red hue fetched the highest prices at the trading markets.

"It could not have just grown there?"

"Nei," Edda whispered. "The plant comes from the west. I have only seen it once before." Ivvár had planted it—there was no other explanation. Where had he found the cutting?

Samara nudged her shoulder. "A rare flower planted amongst the weeds—you are the flower, Edda. It is just as I said—he is wooing you." Samara pointed down at the tiny yellow flowers swaying in the breeze. "This. Is. Seduction."

Seduction. The word froze in her mind. This flower was yet another move in Ivvár fulfilling his promise to win her favor.

"What an awful husband," Samara said, her tone playful.

Edda frowned. *I am no flower, not beautiful.*

Samara clapped delightedly, oblivious to her inner turmoil. "He planted it for you to find. You should go to him. Thank him."

"Now?" It was a thoughtful gift, yet she did not wish to encourage his affection. She would prefer he turned his attention to seeking out another woman for his bed.

"Já, now. Though neither of you chose this marriage, he is your husband, and you cannot keep ignoring him."

Samara spoke true, Ivvár had been forced into this marriage too, but unlike her, he was attempting to make the union work. Was she being unfair in her treatment of him? "I cannot bed him. I should not encourage him."

"Bah!" Samra waved her hand dismissively. "The priestess is mistaken. Bedding a man cannot drain a magic woman of her power. Go to him."

Was Alva wrong? She was a powerful völva, yet had never lain with a man herself. Where had the tale of the curse

begun? Was it merely a myth embellished with age to keep
wayward völva from straying in their devotion to the gods?

"Edda?"

Edda released a heavy sigh. Now she felt more confused
than ever.

"At least thank him for the gift," Samara said.

Edda stared down at her bare feet and considered the
quandary. She did not want to embolden Ivvár's wooing, yet
it would be poor manners not to acknowledge the generous
gift.

With one hand pressed to her lower back, Samara made
her way toward the bench seat at the end of the row of
garden beds. "Ivvár has gone to much trouble to find such a
precious plant for your garden."

Edda hastened after Samara, aiding her friend down onto
the seat before lowering herself beside her. "After our visit, I
will find Ivvár and thank him."

Samara smiled brightly. "Very good. Now tell me what
you have planned next for your garden."

CHAPTER TWELVE

EDDA

*E*dda passed by the old stone well, her toes curling
into the thick grass underfoot as she entered the
garden she had avoided since arriving on Gottland. She
stepped forward, intent on offering her thanks and leaving
Ivvár to his day.

Simple.

A high wall wrapped around all sides, the weather-worn
limestone providing protection from the blustering winds
and privacy from the bustling village outside. Her gaze swept
over the newly planted garden beds nestled along one side of
the wall and the orchard of freshly pruned apple trees on the
other. This garden would provide much of the stores needed
to get the clan through the long winters when in full harvest.

Blessed Freya! Edda stumbled to a halt at the vision
before her.

Ivvár lofted the ax over his head, a small rivulet of sweat
dripping down the center of his bare back to the top of his
pants. Muscles rippled as he splintered the wood into two
halves with a swift swing.

Edda swallowed hard. A warrior body was often on display at court, yet Ivvár was different. He was not a stranger. He was the first man she had ever known, talked with, been angry with...

Kissed.

She had been telling herself the kiss meant naught, but it was a lie she no longer believed now that she could feel his nearness with every beat of her heart. This bond between them was more than she had ever felt.

Much more.

Any man could coax a response from a woman's body, but it wasn't just any man she ached for, and it wasn't just those parts of her body made for passion. Nei. She felt an uncomfortable ache in her heart whenever she looked into his stormy blue eyes.

"That is the last of it, Kal. You did well. Now go home and be back here at dawn," her husband said.

A lanky boy stepped into view, nodding at Ivvár before collecting the split wood.

Edda watched Ivvár place his hand on the boy's shoulder, hesitant to make herself known. She liked seeing him like this, at ease. Being back in this garden had settled some of the restless energy she'd noticed when they'd met.

"You did well." Ivvár ruffled the boy's hair.

His kindness warmed her heart. This was a different Ivvár, not Ivvár the warrior, brother, or husband. This was the true Ivvár when he was not hiding behind his affable charm and not being watched. He looked confident, capable, and happy. He was dangerous to her like this, sober and in control. Now that she thought on it, she could not remember the last time she'd seen him drink more than one mug of ale. With each passing day of fulfilling his duty, his confidence seemed to grow.

A glow of pride lit the young boy's face.

Edda stepped forward. "Ivvár."

Ivvár spun around, a grin splitting his face when he saw her. "You can go now, Kal." As he spoke, his gaze remained locked on her.

Kal cast her a curious look as he passed by her with his load of firewood.

"You came," Ivvár said, drawing her attention back to him as he closed the distance between them.

"I did."

"Why?" His gaze lingered on the eagle feathers painted on her cheeks. He'd become increasingly curious about her changing masks and even teased her each night with guesses for the following day.

"I came to see your garden."

Ivvár raised an eyebrow at her. "Hmm." Collecting his shirt from a fallen stump, he wiped the glistening sweat from his brow and the front of his chest.

Her eyes followed his every move. "You have a new helper?" she asked, eager to break the uncomfortable silence.

"Já. Kal has much to learn, but he works hard." Ivvár reached out and slid his hand into hers. "Come. I will show you what we have done."

Her breath caught at his firm grip as he tugged her forward.

When they stopped in the shade of an apple tree, Ivvár released her hand and tossed his damp shirt over a branch. Dappled sunlight filtered through the thick blossoms covering the gnarled branches that reached in a tangled mess in all directions.

Resting a hand on the rough tree bark, Edda closed her eyes and paused to breathe in the light, sweet scent and listen to the twittering of a lark soaring overhead. The life source of the ancient tree called to her, vibrated beneath her palm. Powerful magic dwelt here—she could feel the ritual offerings of many generations of völva that had seeped into the earth. This was a sacred garden formed through the unbroken devotion and reverence of those entrusted with its care and protection. Did Ivvár know that?

Her question faded when she opened her eyes.

Ivvár stood with his head tilted back, the muscles in his powerful neck moving as he drank from his waterskin.

Gods! He was magnificent. All the Eriksson brothers were handsome, but only Ivvár made her heart pound or her body burn.

After securing the wooden stopper on the leather waterskin, Ivvár placed it at the tree's base and offered his hand again. "We can begin at the herb beds."

Speak. Leave. For a moment, she was conflicted, her path unclear, before she forged on.

"I did not come to see the garden."

Meeting her gaze, Ivvár stepped closer. "You did not?"

Edda stumbled back against the tree trunk, her hands pressing against the bark. He was too close, too virile, too everything. "Nei. I…" She could barely force the words out. "I found the flower. It is lovely. My thanks."

Ivvár closed the distance between them with one quick step and placed one hand beside her head, his gaze holding her captive. "You did?" His deep growl made her heart skip.

"Já," Edda whispered, continuing before she lost her nerve. "Why did you turn my garden beds? I told you to stay out of my garden."

Ivvár dipped his head closer, his breath hot on her ear as he whispered. "It pleases me to please you, wife."

A shiver wracked her body. This was Ivvár the charmer—seducing with the same ease as breathing, his every muscle taut with anticipation as he waited for the slightest sign of a weakness he could exploit. Within her, something quivered, unfurled from the shadows in the recesses of her being. She wanted to surrender, to relinquish the heavy layers of stone that encased her heart, and to know what it would be like to be vulnerable and trust a man once more. Afraid he would see her weakness with one glance at her eyes, she turned away. He was so close that her lips brushed against his bare shoulder.

Ivvár stiffened.

Neither of them moved.

His palm cradled her head, his lips slowly descending.

Her eyes fluttered closed. And then his arm was around her waist, crushing her to him. Her lips parted with a breathy sigh, and she leaned into the caress, shifted against him, and melted.

Soft lips covered hers hungrily, demanding and deliberate in their dominance.

Bliss.

The whimpers of encouragement that escaped her seemed only to fuel his hunger. His hands were everywhere, her shoulders, her breasts, the nape of her neck, tangled in her hair as he cupped the back of her head and slowed the kiss.

Warm, sweet bliss.

Sparks of light flickered beneath her closed eyelids as he lifted her leg and wrapped it around his waist, his hard length pressing against her soft core.

Edda gasped and tore her lips from his, breathing quick and shallow.

Moving his attention, Ivvár nuzzled at her neck.

The brush of his stubble and hot kisses against her tender

flesh made her throw her head back in ecstasy. Tilting her head, she let him have his way.

"Gods, Edda. You undo me," he growled, rocking against her.

Her heart pounded wildly, drowning out the keening moan that escaped her lips as her hands clutched him. Every breath, every touch, every brush of his lips tore down another stone from the fortress around her heart. Until all that was left was him.

Ivvár.

Her hands clawed at the scaly bark, her back arching as a surge of earthy power crashed over her, stealing the air from her lungs. She rocked against him, desperately climbing, seeking.

Holding her tight, Ivvár matched her rhythm with each thrust of his hips. In hushed whispers, he told her that he would hold her, protect her, give her what she needed, and that she was what he needed. Then his hand cupped her breast, his deft fingers gently plucking at her furled nipple.

Crying out, she gripped his forearms, warmth exploding within her as she shattered.

Soared.

Her senses honed as the spark of her magic flared, as she felt the unmistakable sensation of it firing in her blood. Her breath caught, and she pulled away.

But Ivvár's brawny arms tightened to prevent her withdrawal, and he held her face buried against his chest as she caught her breath. And blessed Freya, it felt wonderful to have someone hold her. Not someone. Him. But as the heady sensation waned, she bit her lip. Her magic had surged with more power than she'd ever felt before.

Was it possible that Alva was wrong?

"Look at me." Ivvár's hand found hers, and he twined their fingers together.

Nei! She was too vulnerable. Her thoughts whirled. She needed time, time to understand. What if she was confused, and her connection to her magic had disappeared in that surge?

Her eyes opened and met blue ones consumed by scorching desire.

Ivvár wanted her.

The wind gusted, rattling through the branches overhead and sending a shower of apple blossom petals falling around them.

"I need you," Ivvár said and then swept his thumb across her lips and down her cheek before holding it up in front of her face.

The smeared clay and powder on his thumb made her heart race.

"I need all of you. Show me."

All desire faded, replaced by the familiar painful bite of self-doubt as she shook her head. "I cannot." Ivvár would not want her when he saw her unmasked. No man would. She couldn't change that, but she could keep him from discovering her secret.

Hurt flashed in his eyes as he stepped back.

An overwhelming urge to wash away the paint, to bare herself to him in all her ugliness, almost brought her to her knees. It had been a mistake to waver in her resolve to keep him at a distance, a terrible mistake.

"I cannot," she whispered. Looking down at the ground, she braced herself for his anger. The anger she could bear—it was the rejection that would follow that would hurt.

"I need you, all of you. But I'll not bed you unless you desire it, until you willingly give all of yourself."

Her mind recoiled at his words, all her fear that he would shun her slipping away like an ebbing tide.

His fingers were gentle as he cupped her chin tenderly and lifted her head until their eyes locked. "Someday, you will take it off, Edda. And I will be waiting.

CHAPTER THIRTEEN

IVVÁR

*I*vvár sidestepped a large man followed by his three burly sons and hastened through the bustling market after his wife. His stomach rumbled at the scent of spices and roasting boar. Ivvár cast a longing look at a band of warriors down an ale as they ate their fill. He'd forgotten the delicacies that made their way to Visby on the trading ships—juicy citrus fruits from the arid isles of the middle sea, sweet treats made from cinnamon, cardamom, and other spices from the east.

"Hurry, Ivvár," Edda ordered, glancing over her shoulder at him impatiently. Turning away, she continued weaving through stalls and past villagers acquiring goods before the traders departed at dawn on the favorable winds.

"Edda, must you buy something from every stall?" This was the most painful kind of torture. He would never have agreed to grant her a favor had he known he would become a packhorse.

The tips of her fiery curls bounced against the enticing curve of her bottom as she moved through the market with the same merciless determination as before. "There is much I need, Ivvár. So many of the traders have seeds and plants."

"Not anymore," he muttered, looking down at the load of packages and seedlings in his arms.

Edda skidded to a stop and turned on her heel to face him. Her hands settled on her hips, and she narrowed her eyes at him. "Are you complaining?"

Ivvár shook his head. "A wise man knows when to be quiet."

Edda eyed him suspiciously.

"Even if his arms ache," he said with a wink.

The corners of her lips twitched and curved upward. "Poor husband, so many muscles, yet you tire easily." Edda winked cheekily before turning and walking away.

"Why you…" He chased after her, grinning at her laughter as she hurried through the market, intent on escape. He liked this playful side of her. It felt like a genuine affection akin to what his parents had.

When Edda discovered the woad he'd planted in her garden, something had shifted between them, and he was glad for it. She had taken to visiting him and Kal in the village garden, and this morn, she had asked him to sow plants in *her* garden.

"What shall we sow first?" he asked as they walked through the village toward home. The fates had chosen well to send him a wife that shared his passion for growing plants. She knew as much as he of the healing kinds, which preferred sunlight or shade, liked their roots deep, or could survive a late frost.

Edda pushed open the wooden gate. "Mayhap the shepherd's purse and chamomile. I have much need for them both. And then the fennel seeds and meadowsweet. What do you think?"

Ivvár followed her into the garden. He liked that he could talk to her about what he loved, and looked forward to their evenings swapping ideas over a simple meal. He lowered the various cuttings and packages of seeds to the ground carefully. "We shall do as you wish. It is your garden."

Edda shook her head and gave him a look of apology. "Nei. It is *our* garden."

Ivvár blinked and then stared at her, speechless. His heart pounded against his ribcage. He knew what those words cost her. Edda had claimed this garden as her private sanctuary from the moment she had arrived on the island. A warm glow spread through his chest at the magnitude of her declaration. She trusted him to care for the plants integral to her work as völva. She would share her sanctuary with *him*.

He smiled at her gently. "Nei, Edda. This is your garden now. I am honored that you asked me to assist with the planting. What changed your mind?"

Her green eyes shone brightly as they rose and met his own. "I have seen your gift, Ivvár, how you honor and care for the village garden. It is your calling, just as being völva is mine." She looked away as though his gaze made her uncomfortable. "Besides, I would be glad for someone to turn the beds for me each spring."

Ivvár retrieved the spade leaning against the wall and returned to stand in front of her. "And to admire your brawny bare-chested husband?"

"Oh, hush!" Her cheeks flushed a charming shade of pink. "Start digging the holes over there…" She pointed at a fallow bed to her right. "And I shall chase away all of your admirers."

Chuckling, Ivvár made his way to the garden bed and began turning the soil. This battle of wits between them only made him want to win her favor more.

"Edda?"

"Já." She looked up from where she knelt, sorting the seedlings they needed.

"Would you do the mid-summer ritual in the village garden?" It was what Lasse would have wanted. He had neglected the rituals that honored the gods and ensured the successful harvest needed to feed his clan for far too long.

She smiled at him gently. "I would be honored."

Satisfied, he returned to digging. Now that he felt settled back in the village and at ease with his marriage, he was not certain he should seduce Edda. He could not want to risk destroying this friendship they had formed. Losing her connection to the gods and her magic would be a devastating blow for Edda. He didn't want his wife to look at him and be reminded of all she had lost. He knew well that resentment spread like a sickness, infecting everything it touched.

Would bedding his wife ruin his marriage?

CHAPTER FOURTEEN

IVVÁR

*I*vvár swung around at the sudden creaking shudder of the old wooden cart rocking on its axle behind him. Letting the ax fall harmlessly to his side, he looked at Kal.

"What are you doing?"

Kal huffed, his whole body tensing as he grunted and kicked the cart's wheel, causing another groaning jolt. "Per needs to empty the cart. He is too slow."

Ivvár leaned the ax against a tree and peered into the cart filled with cuttings and weeds. There was no reason for such a reaction. More debris could be piled on top without overloading the sturdy axles. Another fit of temper from the boy —the third of the day.

"Kal, you know Per is busy with his crops. You can empty it. A boy your age should be able to use a cart."

Kal thrust out his chest, his eyes narrowing. "I shouldn't have to. Per promised he would come."

"You shall empty it and then finish your work," he said in a firm tone, wondering why Kal was being so disagreeable.

The boy usually never complained about anything he was asked to do.

"Gods! Does nobody honor their word?" Kal stamped his foot, his fists clenching so tight his knuckles turned white.

Ivvár studied the boy he had come to know well over these past weeks. He could see the turmoil in Kal's expression and feel his frustration. This outburst was not about Per or the cart—it was about something else entirely.

"How fares your father?" He should have thought to ask after Baldr sooner.

Kal kicked at the dirt at his feet, sending up a cloud of dust. "Much pleased for the extra coin I bring home."

"Did you embrace him?"

"Já."

"And?"

Kal shook his head and looked away.

Ivvár rubbed his beard, the dull ache in the back of his throat growing. Clearly, it had not gone well. He knew the feeling of watching someone you cared for suffering—and how it hurt when they would rather keep their pain than accept your aid. The pain of that rejection eventually crumbled your belief in the bonds between men because, without trust, there was no brotherhood. And if Rorik had taught him anything, it was that the despair that came with losing someone you loved oozed into everything in your life. Kal did not deserve that—nobody did. His frustration swelled. He knew Valen had called on Baldr and offered work tanning hides, but the warrior had yet to respond.

"You can tell me. It will stay between us." It was admirable that Kal did not want to speak ill of his father, but ignoring his anger would hurt him more.

Tears welled in the boy's eyes as he spoke. "He pushed me away and demanded my coin."

Ivvár's temper flared. Baldr was so deep in his cups that he had no notion of how he hurt his son. Where many would have forsaken a man broken by war and injury, Kal had stayed. But if Baldr continued down this path, eventually, even Kal would abandon his father.

Kal wiped the tears from his face and straightened his shoulders.

"Sometimes a man struggles to speak about his worries, to face himself."

Like Rorik.

"Your father has only ever been a warrior. Now he is injured and must discover who he is without his sword." Ivvár reached out, wanting to console the boy.

Kal shoved his hand away. "Just tell me how to fix it," he demanded.

"I cannot. It is not so…"

Turning on his heel, Kal almost stumbled over his feet in his haste to escape.

"Simple," Ivvár muttered under his breath as the boy disappeared in the direction of the village. Closing his eyes, he released a heavy sigh. He would visit Baldr himself and knock sense into the man if need be.

"Do they all run from you like that?"

Ivvár spun around.

Rorik.

His twin sat atop the limestone wall that ran along the back of the garden, arms folded across his chest, watching him.

"How long have you been there?" Ivvár balled his fingers into fists, the tips brushing against his blistered palms.

Rorik smirked. "Long enough to see the whelp cry and run away like a mouse."

"The boy is brave—he speaks of his troubles—unlike you."

Ivvár opened his senses, needing to feel the bond, something he could push against.

Naught.

Rorik jumped to the ground, his gaze narrowing. "You have something to say?"

"Do you, *brother*? Will you tell me why you push me away? Or why you will not share what made you like this?" They were questions he had asked before, questions he had given up hope of being answered. Admitting that hurt, but he was weary of suffocating in this whirlpool of darkness and secrets with someone who did not want to live. His torment ended now. This was the last time he would ever ask these questions. Whether or not his twin gave him answers, he would swim to the surface and save himself.

"Naught happened," Rorik snapped, surlier than a cornered bear.

"Talk to me, brother."

Rorik paced back and forth restlessly. "If I had known you would nag at me, I would not have come."

Ivvár tilted his head and watched his twin. "Why are you here then?"

"I am leaving," Rorik said, stopping suddenly. He closed the distance between them, his stride aggressive and his face so close that their noses almost touched.

Ivvár noted the simmering fury in his brother's eyes. A lesser man would have stepped back. Not he. He was not intimidated by a man afraid to face his troubles.

"Coward," Ivvár muttered, wiping his hands on his pants. Rorik let his fear about whatever had happened in the past control him and used it as an excuse to push everyone that loved him away.

"What did you say?"

Ivvár wiped away Rorik's spittle from his face. "You heard

me. You refuse to discuss your troubles yet make snide remarks about a boy struggling to deal with his wounded father who has turned to drink. You are the mouse, not the boy."

A fist slammed into his cheek, the impact ringing in his head. His lip split open, sending out an arc of splattered blood. Ivvár stumbled backward, his hand wiping away the blood before curling into a fist. Furious, he leaped forward, his arms wrapping around his brother's waist.

Rorik grunted as he slammed into the ground.

Straddling his waist, Ivvár struck hard. They would settle this the way they always had—with fists, blood, and bruises. His body moved in a familiar rhythm—a right hook, a left jab, and a pounding of body shots.

Bucking wildly, Rorik rolled them over and returned the pummeling with one of his own.

Thrusting his head upward, Ivvár heard the satisfying crunch of his forehead hitting bone and Rorik falling off him with a thud. He jumped to his feet quickly, crouching to catch his breath as he watched his brother warily.

Rorik's chest heaved from exertion—his expression thunderous as he rose to his feet. "Never call me *that.*" He spat at the ground in disgust, unable to even speak the word aloud. Coward. It was the worst of insults to a Viking warrior.

Ivvár stood, determined not to back away from this long-overdue battle. "It's true, and you know it. You are too afraid to face your fears—face yourself."

Rorik glowered. "What ails you?"

Saddened that it had come to this, Ivvár shook his head. "I am weary of this battle between us."

"What battle? You hit like a whelp." Rorik's tone was mocking, cold.

It was all the confirmation Ivvár needed. "There is naught between us anymore, Rorik. You are a stranger to me."

Rorik grunted, his expression souring.

"Not once since we returned home have you sought me out." Rorik inhabited an in-between place, not living yet not dead, avoiding people, alone, even in crowds. He had walked beside his twin in that lonely, empty place for years, but not anymore.

Rorik waved a hand dismissively. "I sat with you at the clan feast."

"The feast Valen insisted you attend?" Ivvár threw back. He was through accepting his brother's lies and excuses. Emboldened, he voiced the dark unspoken secret that everyone ignored. "You sat with me to avoid the hushed whispers that follow you."

Rorik stiffened.

A chilled silence surrounded them.

Ivvár thrust the knife deeper into the wound he suspected had made his twin this way, past the point of no return. He had nothing more to lose. "Why do you not defend yourself against the poisonous rumors about Gilda?"

Rorik avoided his gaze.

"Look at me!" Ivvár demanded, years of simmering anger and frustration erupting. "No more hiding, brother. Did you hurt Gilda?"

Whilst Rorik and Gilda had shared furs, accusations had spread like wildfire through the clan. Whispers of beddings that involved ropes, blood, and pain. Unusual appetites were not unheard of or even frowned upon, but when a bruised Gilda had been seen leaving Visby, Rorik had been accused of beating her. His twin had suffered the accusations in silence, not once speaking in his defense. Afeared of his temper and strength, the clan's women had shunned him from their furs forevermore.

Rorik stared back at him, his lips a firm line, unmoving. Ivvár shook his head. "Your silence speaks to your guilt."

Rorik opened his mouth. His jaw moved up and down, yet no sound came out.

"No more secrets, lies, or shutting me out. Refuse me now, and you can be miserable on your own."

The flash of pain in Rorik's eyes shuttered so fast that Ivvár doubted it had even happened.

He knew what came next— this was where Rorik ran, escaped. He had not wanted it to end this way, did not want to deny his twin the lightness that he brought to the bond they shared, but he could not continue this way. Rorik would survive without his light—he did not want it anyway.

Ivvár spoke the words he had never dared before. "If you leave, we are done, brother. I will not follow."

His heart sank as Rorik turned on his heel and walked away without looking back. The last sliver of hope that his twin would choose him, dying.

"Son of Loki!" His fist connected with bark, blood dripping down his knuckles and onto the grass underfoot. Ivvár stomped towards home, furious at himself for caring so much and punishing himself by repeatedly reaching out only to be bitten.

He was through with allowing people to push him away. Rorik. Edda. All he wanted was the truth, to be let in just a little. Gods! He gave all of himself to them, yet anyone he cared for pushed him away. Neither Rorik nor Edda trusted him enough to share their secrets.

With each determined step, he felt the blade fall on his bond with his twin, hacking and slicing until all that remained was a hollowness that reminded him that he would never be whole again.

* * *

Ivvár slammed the door against the wall with a loud crash. Muttering a stream of curses that matched his mood, he caught it before it whacked him in his face on its return and stepped into the steaming bathhouse. He needed to remove the sweat, grime, and misery of the day. His fingers tightened on the wooden door as the sharp scent of birchwood and rosemary added to his jagged nerves.

Edda!

Daylight filtered through the doorway to where she sat perched on the stone ledge in the bath, her red hair a messy tangle of curls piled on her head. Steaming water lapped at her shoulders. Clay of whites, yellows, and browns covered her face, creating the image of a deer with big pale eyes, and the very tip of her nose was smudged with black kohl.

"Oh!" Edda's gasp echoed in the small wooden hut.

Ivvár stilled.

The sight of her bathed in the sunlight streaming through the open door and the light from the lantern hanging from a rafter overhead ignited a war within him. The intricate lines of the carefully applied paint Edda wore were breathtaking. He admired her for remaining fearless and continuing to wear her mask despite judgment from others.

And yet those masks that he so admired, which made her so unlike any women he had ever known, were the very thing she used as a weapon to keep him away. Now that he understood her better, he knew he would never truly know his wife until that paint came off.

"I-I can go," Edda stammered, looking at him wide-eyed.

"Do. Not. Move," he said and closed the door, sliding the latch into place. Rorik had escaped him, scampering away to his hut in the forest. He could not bear to have Edda run from him too.

Her green eyes stared up at him for a heartbeat before she nodded.

His head bumped the lantern as he crossed to the bath, sending muted light flickering across the walls until he stopped it from swaying.

All the while, Edda lay submerged in the water, her gaze a firestorm burning a path of destruction across his skin. She devastated him without trying or even wanting to, like no other woman ever had. Edda made him obsessed, needy. Her thoughts invaded his every waking moment and kept him up through the night. He was…

Bewitched.

Yet he would not surrender. He would not continue to allow her to make him vulnerable without fighting back. He wanted her to feel like he did, to be so enamored that she too was at the mercy of this maddening tempest.

"I will undress. Turn away if that offends you." Reaching down, he gripped the hem of his shirt and pulled it up over his head.

Edda's gaze slid down over his chest and stomach, then back up to meet his.

Good. He would not hold back or hide his body from her anymore. After placing the shirt on the hook beside her dress, he removed his pants and hung them.

His eyes returned to her.

Still, she watched him, a red flush creeping up her neck, but her gaze held.

Their eyes locked as he crossed to the bath.

Edda leaned back and waited—her demeanor wary. He

knew she'd sensed the shift in him, saw the difference in how he approached her, and wondered what it meant.

Ivvár lowered himself into the bath beside her, the warm water doing naught to calm the angst rushing through his veins. Kal, the fight with Rorik, this constant tension in his marriage—he felt like he was at sea in a storm without a sail. He could not trust himself to remain calm, that the anger he was feeling would not scorch everything it touched. He did not want to damage another relationship, not after how things had ended with Rorik.

"It is best that you leave, Edda," he said in a tone that brooked no argument. He leaned back until the water lapped at his chest and closed his eyes. Slowly, he filled his lungs and then exhaled, focusing on the rhythm of his breath rather than the churning in his gut. Deep down, he'd long known he would lose Rorik and had expected that loss's pain even, but not like this. He never expected that he would be the one abandoning his twin and feeling the accompanying guilt of that betrayal. Or that he would be left suffering like a wounded warrior alone and forsaken on the battlefield. *How had it come to this?*

Water splashed around him—Edda leaving. He tamped down the twinge of disappointment. The further she was from him, the safer she would be.

Warm water cascaded over his scalp. His eyes flew open.

Edda sat beside him, pouring a pitcher of water over his head, her bared breasts tantalizingly close to his mouth.

"Lean back. Close your eyes." A firm whisper, eyes that challenged him to disobey.

Lowering his lashes, he let his body sink into the water. Somehow, she had understood that he needed her. With a long, exhausted sigh, he relaxed. Being naked around him would surely make Edda nervous, and she knew it would be wise to leave, yet she had chosen not to forsake him. Mayhap it was the healer in her sensing his turmoil, his need for companionship? Whatever it was, he was glad not to be alone.

A comforting silence settled softly between them.

Edda's fingertips slid across his scalp, working the rosemary-scented soap into a lather.

Never had he been touched with such familiarity by a woman not his kin without expectation. In his experience, they all wanted something in return—either to be bedded by the wild Eriksson brother or to convince him to use his family connections for their benefit. Sometimes they'd wanted both. He'd often obliged to satisfy his need to feel connected to someone, even for a short while. Yet a thread of dishonesty tainted such encounters and had him leaving those beds feeling even more lonely.

The gentle press of Edda's fingers in his hair eased the tension from his body.

Her touch was entirely different from those before—innocent and sincere in its intention to provide comfort and healing. His cock jumped in response to the precious connection. Gods, he wanted her more than air itself. Everything she did made him want her—watching her abandon everything to rush to heal someone, coming home to a house that smelt like fresh-cut herbs, even the overwhelming number of rune sticks that had overtaken the cottage garden. He was drawn to the beauty and honesty that radiated from within her, longed to feel her pressed against him and hear the breathy moans that told him he affected her. He yearned to feel that undeniable connection when they kissed, that melding of two becoming one.

Water splashed and ran down his face as Edda rinsed the soap from his hair.

Ivvár lifted his lashes and looked up at her. He did not attempt to hide the hunger he knew blazed in his eyes. This was him, and he would no longer temper and hide his truth to appease others. He would no longer shy away from his desires—if Edda could not abide the warrior and man he was, he would rather know it now.

Arm outstretched, she stilled as the water trickled from the wooden bowl onto his head. She stared at him for a few moments, and he sensed her mind racing. How would she react to his desire for her?

Her jaw jutted, her gaze holding his, bold, unashamed.

Edda's silent acquiescence confirmed his suspicions, and his heart leaped, a lightness filling his chest.

She wanted him.

The air thickened between them, heavy with the primal allure of their mutual yearning.

He reached for her, aware of the rhythmic pulse of their hearts beating in tandem the moment his fingers encircled her wrist. Gently, he took the bowl from her hand and set it aside.

"Come." When she did not protest, he tugged gently.

She rocked back and forth for a moment as though undecided before toppling forward in surrender.

Catching her as she glided through the water, Ivvár wrapped an arm around her waist and settled her on his lap with the hard evidence of his desire pressed against her behind.

Edda shuddered in his arms. "I—"

"Not that," he reassured her. "I will have you desperate, needy, and begging when we join. For now, all I want is to show you pleasure." Slowly, he moved his hand upward. Her skin was soft and silky, her stomach firm. He rested his hand between her breasts.

Her head fell back against his shoulder as she sagged against him. Her eyes were closed, her breathing steady and unafraid.

He pressed a gentle kiss to her lips.

She whimpered.

Emboldened, he lifted his other hand and gently cupped her breast, delighting in her throaty moan of approval. This he could do for his wife—give her pleasure, show her the joys of release. He dipped his other hand beneath the water and between her thighs, his fingers seeking out and parting her flesh as he probed for the place at the core of her pleasure.

"Ohh!" Her back arched when he found it, her hips rising as he rubbed in a circular motion.

A satisfied smile curved his lips, his fingers maintaining the constant ebb and flow of hard, then soft, to keep her on the edge of release.

Edda was limp in his embrace, one arm rising to wrap around the back of his neck—her nakedness long forgotten.

He gazed down at her furled nipples thrusting upward with each panting breath, overcome with emotion at the trust she had relinquished to him. He would fall on his sword rather than betray her faith in him.

Holding her close, he nuzzled her neck, placing first gentle kisses and then playful nips on the soft skin. She tasted sweet, like the sprigs of rosemary she had added to the warm bathwater.

Humming approvingly, Edda pressed back against his touch. Her head fell to the side until her cheek rested on his chest.

Holding her in his arms with this newfound under-standing between them felt sacred and otherworldly. And every part of him knew that they were fated, that Edda was his, and he hers. Dipping his head, he claimed her mouth in a possessive kiss, relief sweeping through him at her eager surrender. He slid his fingers lower.

With a gasp, she broke from the kiss. Her hands clamped down on his forearm, her nails digging into his flesh.

"Breathe, little wife." Sliding his hands beneath her bottom, Ivvár lifted and spun her around to face him. Careful to avoid placing her near his rigid manhood, he set her down on his thighs.

She stiffened—her grip still firm on his arm—her gaze wary.

Water splashed as he leaned forward, touching his forehead to hers, and stared deep into her eyes. He was loath to frighten her yet unwilling to let her withdraw from him, not when she was finally letting him in. "Let me show you, Edda."

Slowly her fingers released their grip, and he lifted her hand and held it against his chest. "I'll not hurt you. I swear it."

"I believe you." The soft rasp of her voice was like sweet music to his ears.

His mind, his senses, reeled. Letting his eyes roam over her figure, he committed to memory everything about this moment—the warmth of the water, the light from the lantern flickering across her skin, the sensation of her thighs brushing against his. Until his last breath, he would never forget the sight of her plump breasts and dusky pink nipples peeking through the wild auburn curls that had fallen loose with the tips trailing in the water lapping at her waist.

"Kiss me," he said, needing to know that she wanted this as much as he did.

Edda leaned forward and pressed her lips against his, firm, restrained.

Sliding a hand up to cradle the back of her head, he urged her to tilt her head and then deepened the kiss, lingering, savoring.

Edda whimpered in approval, then responded with a reckless abandon that made his blood heat. *Intoxicating.* He moved his fingers between her thighs and then lower.

She rocked into his hand, needing the friction of his touch.

The kiss turned frenzied, his fingers exploring further. He resisted the urge to roar in approval when her hips thrust forward again. It was the sign he had been awaiting. He took control and commanded her body as he guided her toward release.

Soon Edda jerked in his arms and broke the kiss, her forehead falling against his chest. She was close, teetering on the precipice of rapture.

"Já. Feel what it does to you." He thrust faster, his other hand plucking at her furled nipples as his mouth returned to her neck. "Feel what I do to you."

Her breathing ragged, Edda writhed against his ministrations.

Ivvár pulled her closer until her soft folds met his rigid member. Guiding her hips, he encouraged her to rock against him, offering the friction she needed without claiming her body.

Her lips parted in a breathy sigh as she found her rhythm, her body moving in the sensual dance as primal and ancient as the gods themselves.

Sliding an arm around her waist, he pressed his mouth to her ear and whispered, "Let go, little wife. I shall catch you."

"Ivvár!" Her body bowed, her head falling back as she soared.

He groaned as she shuddered against his aching cock, the

tips of her hair teasing his thighs. He craved her with a hunger he could feel in every heartbeat. His balls ached with the need to claim her, to lose himself in her velvety warmth.

As the stupor of satisfaction overtook her, he gathered her close. "Rest now," he said, his hands languidly moving up and down her back.

Releasing a shuddering sigh, she snuggled against his chest. And then, as her breathing slowed, she tilted her head back and looked up at him. "You confuse me, Ivvár. Most men ask for more of a woman."

"I am not most men." He held her firmly against his chest, feeling victorious in his efforts to win her over.

"You do not want me?"

"Can you not feel my response? I want you more than anything, Edda." Though he had felt her surrender to their connection, she was still hiding from him and keeping secrets. He wrapped an arm around her as she snuggled closer. He wanted his wife more than he had ever wanted a woman, but he found little joy in a half-won prize.

"I want all of you."

CHAPTER FIFTEEN

EDDA

*T*wo nights later, Edda settled Söl's dish on the ground and glided her fingers through the cat's soft fur as Ivvár strode through the doorway with a cloth wrapped around his waist and a handful of soiled clothes. His bare chest was broad and devoid of a single hair to mar the sun-bronzed expanse. Her fingers tingled with a reckless urge to explore the ridges and valleys of muscle, to feel the vitality of his heart beating and the strength and warmth of his flesh.

A contented purr vibrated beneath her fingertips, pulling her from her musings. "Good boy, Söl. Did you chase off those mice?" she cooed, scratching behind his ears.

"If you keep overfeeding him, he will never hunt." Ivvár shook his head, his damp hair scattering a shower of droplets as he strode past her and tossed the clothes in the woven basket.

Edda stared at him. Ivvár barely noticed when she admired his body, mayhap because he was accustomed to women fawning over him, so she had long ceased hiding it.

He was a commanding presence at any time, but only when unclothed was the true masculine power of his body revealed —broad shoulders, lean muscular legs, and rippling bulging muscles everywhere.

"He will hunt when he feels settled in his home." When they had first wed, she had been too wary of the mighty warrior who could easily overpower her to argue back. But now she knew Ivvár's affable nature and that, even if they disagreed, he would not hurt her.

Somehow, that was worse.

More dangerous.

She could loathe and curse a man who beat her or forced her to bend to his will, but there was no defense against kindness and patience. Even worse, and much to her chagrin, her magic had begun to dim when they were too long apart. She did not even want to contemplate the reasons behind that worrying occurrence.

Ivvár placed his hands on his hips and stared down at her with a teasing twinkle in his eyes. "He will hunt when you stop feeding him and treating him like a babe."

Söl's back arched, his hackles rising as he hissed in Ivvár's direction.

Edda stood upright, shaking her head at the tension between her two housemates. "He may warm to you if you stop moving him to the basket on the floor at night."

"And I will warm to him when I am not waking to find him curled up at my feet."

"He likes to be near me."

Ivvár glared down at Söl, who was licking the empty dish. "I'll not share my bed with an animal."

Edda pressed her lips together, refusing to reply when his gaze returned to her again. There was naught left to say. Never was there a cat more stubborn and willful than Söl.

Ivvár would soon realize that he was in a battle of wills that he would not win.

"A rabbit feeding a cat," Ivvár said, looking at her face pointedly. "It is no wonder the animal is confused."

"He is not confused, just…misunderstood."

Ivvár guffawed and crossed his arms over his chest.

He did not understand her bond with her cat—that when she thought her sister was dead and her father had abandoned her, Söl had been her constant companion, her family. Something caught her eye. "Is that blood? You are injured."

Ivvár looked at his arm, a frown creasing his forehead at the sight of the blood oozing down his arm from a cut on his shoulder.

Edda crossed to him hastily and examined the wound after using a cloth to wipe away the blood. "How did this happen? You should have come to me at once."

Ivvár shrugged dismissively. "It is but a scratch from a branch."

Her temper flared. Ivvár knew better than to leave a cut unattended. "Even the smallest of wounds can fester. You are a warrior, so do not tell me you do not know this."

Ivvár looked sheepish. "Já. I have known less to kill a man."

Staring up at him, Edda gave him her best scolding glare. "Tell me, who would seek out a healer whose own husband died from a mere cut?"

"Nobody who wanted to live." Ivvár gave her that boyish grin he so often wielded with devastating accuracy.

Edda pushed him toward the table. "This is serious, Ivvár. Your foolishness threatens my place here with the clan. Now sit down, and I will tend it."

"Apologies, Edda. I meant no harm." The lightness disappeared from his eyes as he sat at the table.

Edda walked to the bench strewn with her supplies. Her mind emptied of all else as she prepared the ingredients for a poultice in a small wooden bowl, her hands moving swiftly as she chanted incantations and mixed the concoction of herbs and oils from various jars. After wiping her hands on her apron, she tore strips of unsoiled cloth. Arms laden, she rounded the hearth and placed her supplies on the table.

Ivvár sat leaning forward in the chair with his forearms resting on his thighs, looking down at his hands.

Something troubled him. The longer they lived together, the more she noticed these moments when he seemed to disappear inside himself. There was a darkness he grappled with that she sensed in the heaviness of his thoughts. His moods had been somber these last few days, his demeanor more distant, sad.

Lifting the lid from a cauldron of water simmering over the hearth, she tossed in handfuls of dried herbs and then an onion to aid healing. All the while, she murmured, "Eir, blessed Norn of the healing, I beseech you to aid this man. Take his pain. Heal this wound."

"What say you?"

"A spell." Edda ladled the steaming brew into a small bowl and moved back to the table.

Ivvár leaned back in his chair, his red hair glowing in the firelight.

Edda placed the bowl on the table and turned to face him. "You must not move."

He raised an eyebrow at her curiously. "Must healing be such somber work?"

She dipped a cloth in the pungent brew. The wound needed to be cleaned before spreading the poultice and bandaging the shoulder. "Já. It is necessary when failure means death. Us völva must do all we can to avoid the burden of death weighing on our hearts." She pressed the cloth to the open wound, gently wiping the blood drying around the edges.

Ivvár stiffened. "Gods, woman."

Casting him a bemused smile, she continued at her task. "It will hurt less if you talk to me. Tell me about the garden. Why was it overgrown?"

Ivvár eyed her warily. "My friend, Lasse, planted the garden. When he died four summers ago, I was entrusted to care for it."

"Yet you abandoned it," she said as she turned away to dip the cloth in the poultice, careful to keep any hint of accusation from her tone. She wanted to keep him talking, to learn as much as she could about her husband, who seemed intent on learning all he could about her past while sharing naught of his own.

"I have been raiding with Rorik in the summers," he said gruffly.

Edda kept her eyes on his wound, feigning nonchalance when in truth, she was overjoyed that he had answered. "Lasse taught you about plants and how to grow them?"

"Já. Since I was a boy."

Lightness filled her chest when his tone gentled at her innocuous question. She scraped her teeth across her lower lip to keep from smiling. Her gentle approach was working.

"I imagine that you and Rorik chased trouble together as boys?"

"Já. We were close once."

Though she knew the answer, she asked anyway, curious to hear his response. "You are not close now?"

Hurt flashed in his eyes. "Nei."

"Why?" Edda kept her tone soft, coaxing.

The chair legs scraped on the floor as Ivvár made to rise to his feet.

Placing a hand on his shoulder, she pushed him back down. "Do. Not. Move." She would not allow him to escape now when she was finally getting to the heart of the matter.

Ivvár grunted his displeasure before falling back into the chair. His eyes remained averted in an attempt to hide his secrets from her.

Lifting the threaded needle, Edda began to suture the wound with careful looping knots.

Ivvár grimaced as the metal pierced his skin but uttered no sound.

To heal a heart wound, she must know the root of the problem. The rift between her husband and his brother was dire, yet she sensed that while it bothered Ivvár greatly, the fracture was not the cause of Rorik's darkness. The gods had shown her that light would not shine on the twins' path until Rorik had conquered his darkness—the brothers' fates and happiness were entwined. Ivvár would not be truly happy until they could heal whatever bothered Rorik. Though she was confident she could discover what ailed Rorik eventually, it would be faster if Ivvár told her willingly.

"What is this discord between you and Rorik?"

"I know not." His tone was harsh, clipped.

"You must know something," she probed as she continued to stitch.

"Nei." Ivvár ran a hand through his hair, frustration evident on his face. "Rorik refuses to speak of it."

Her heart ached for him. Ivvár cared about Rorik deeply. And not just his twin, Kal, and her too. Ivvár connected himself to people with a force she would wager could resist even the pull of the highest spring tides. When Ivvár chose you, he gave all of himself—his commitment to love and protect, was absolute. Her heart swelled until it seemed like it would burst out of her chest. He had chosen her.

Her.

Inhaling a deep, calming breath, she returned her focus to the task at hand. "You have asked him?" She carefully tied off the silk thread sutures before placing the needle aside.

"Rorik insists naught is wrong, yet he becomes more distant each year." Ivvár's voice cracked under the weight of the admission.

Edda tipped a tincture from one of her bottles onto a cloth and wiped away the last of his blood.

Ivvár released a shuddering sigh.

"And that pains you?" She placed a hand on his shoulder. Had he ever spoken about his troubles with Rorik aloud? Likely not. In her experience, men unburdened themselves of their troubles far less often than womenfolk.

"We were once close, but I have almost forgotten how that feels." Ivvár's muscles tensed and then relaxed beneath her fingers.

He'll not speak more. As the thought crossed her mind, she knew it to be true. The softening of Ivvár's lips and the slightly relaxed slump of his shoulders confirmed it. When had she become so attuned to him, so aware of his person, his thoughts even?

"Edda?" His voice sounded far away.

Blood rushed to her head, and her knees threatened to give out. How had she not noticed? Somehow, the person she'd been and her life before she wed Ivvár had slowly faded and given way to this new life on the island. She enjoyed being völva for the Eriksson clan and found contentment in settling in the village and having her own home. She had ceased wishing for her old life without even realizing it. This island, this clan, Ivvár, had become her new life.

"Edda?" His brow furrowed downward.

Edda forced a smile and dipped her fingers into the poultice. "Já. I am sorry for you and Rorik." The astringent aroma of herbs assaulted her nostrils as she covered the wound in the healing salve.

"I do not want your pity." He looked affronted.

"And yet you have it. Losing family is the worst of fates." She wound a long strip of cloth around his arm. "Especially when they still breathe."

Warm fingers wrapped around her right arm. Lifting her gaze, Edda looked into eyes filled with sympathy.

Ivvár's thumb brushed across her skin, sending heat coursing through her veins. "It must have been hard losing Ásta and then discovering that she still lived years later."

Her teeth pressed against her bottom lip. His compassion made her want to crawl into his lap and feel his arms around her. How had they led lives so distant and yet so similar? A lump formed in her throat. Of all those that had crossed her path, she'd never have thought that a Viking warrior would be the one to see and understand her. Averting her gaze, she knotted the two ends of the cloth to keep it in place over his wound.

"Did Ásta send word to you while she was hiding in Luleavst?"

"Nei." Swallowing hard, Edda pressed her hand to the sudden stabbing pain in her chest. Despite years of trying, she could not overcome the pain of knowing her sister had not trusted her with the truth.

"Seems we both have thoughtless siblings." Ivvár's fingers enclosed hers with a gentleness that brought tears to her eyes.

Edda pulled her hand away and firmed her resolve. Her past with Ásta could not be undone, but Ivvár and Rorik could still mend their relationship. Somehow, she would find a way to reunite the brothers.

"Stay here. I will bring the night meal."

After returning her supplies to the bench, Edda ladled two hefty servings of stew into bowls and placed them on the table. Though she knew the tension with Rorik bothered Ivvár, she sensed there was more to his dark mood. Was it something she had done?

"It smells good," Ivvár said, picking up his spoon.

Edda lowered herself into the chair across from him and unwrapped the cloth keeping the loaf of bread warm.

He broke off some bread and placed it in front of her before taking his own. His fingers worked deftly, breaking it into smaller pieces that he dipped in the stew and swiftly devoured.

Edda lifted the spoon to her lips. Carefully testing the heat first, she swallowed the rich meaty mouthful. It was good, very good. She would rather be outdoors than inside cooking, but this meal made the day tending the pot over the hearth worthwhile. She looked across at Ivvár eating his meal.

As though he sensed her gaze, Ivvár looked up at her. "Did you see Samara today?"

"Já. Sefa's son fell out of a tree. We went and tended him together."

"Is the boy well?"

"He will be soon. We set the bone. In a few moons, he will run and climb once more."

Ivvár tore off another piece of bread, leaned over, and dipped it in her bowl.

"What are you—"

"Open." When she parted her lips, he placed the food in

her mouth, his thumb brushing against her lower lip when it withdrew.

Her stomach fluttered. *What was he doing?*

He tore another chunk. "How long did you train to become völva?" He fed her again, this time his thumb lingering a little longer.

She swallowed, her confusion growing as she answered. "I was a novice for five summers. This one would have been my second instructing the new novices."

"Eat," he said, motioning at her bowl. "And tell me more of your life with the other völva."

The hearth fire crackled in the background as she told him of Alva, the village in the forest, and training novices. The mealtime passed quickly, Ivvár asking all manner of questions and then listening intently as she answered. Before long, Edda found herself enjoying the easy conversation between them.

Eventually, Ivvár rose to his feet. "My thanks, Edda. That was the first meal you have prepared for me." Smiling at her, he bent and pressed his lips to her forehead. "You please me much, little wife."

Heat warmed her cheeks. She had decided to cook the meal after she had arrived home to find all of her jars of herbs and medicines lined up along a newly built shelf. She knew that no expectation had accompanied his gift, that he had merely seen her need and provided a solution, yet she wanted to repay the kindness.

Ivvár collected both of their bowls and made his way to the bench.

Her eyes followed him as he lifted the pail of water and wiped down their dishes before setting them aside to dry.

As she picked up her mending and watched him, Edda realized an undeniable truth. Little by little, her husband was breaching the barriers she had erected around her heart. She was losing the battle for her affection. Something inside her hoped that Alva had been wrong and that she could have both her magic and Ivvár. She did not want to be forced to choose because she was uncertain what she wanted more— to be völva or lay with her husband.

CHAPTER SIXTEEN

EDDA

*E*dda pulled the thick blankets up to her chin and listened to Ivvár shuffling around beyond the bedchamber. The rough scrape of the wooden bolt lock sliding into place echoed in the silence.

Her stomach fluttered. Soon he would place logs on the hearth fire and join her in their bed. Not long ago, she would have been tense at the mere thought of him lying beside her, but that was before. She no longer feared him. He had proven that he was a man of his word when he could have taken her in the bathhouse yet had not.

The tapestry moved, and Ivvár stepped into their bedchamber. At first, she'd been shocked at the tiny cottage that just the two of them would share, but now she was thankful for the privacy it afforded. She would never have felt comfortable sharing a bed with her husband in a long-house filled with other warriors and their families.

Glancing at her briefly, Ivvár set the lantern beside the bed. "Do you need to go outside? I can leave the lantern alight."

Edda shook her head. "Nei." Ivvár had been sitting by the hearth with his feet up on a stool and whittling away at a piece of oak with his dagger when she'd quietly made her way to the bathhouse for her nightly ablutions. She'd not bothered to ask what he was making, knowing that he liked to be alone with his thoughts when he carved.

Ivvár nodded and began to undress, his movements hurried.

After he had pleasured her in the bathhouse, everything had changed between them. The familiarity she'd felt tending his wound, their easy conversation over the evening meal, and that kiss on the forehead meant she could no longer lie to herself that Ivvár was a stranger. She knew him as a woman knows her husband—knew that he wanted to be alone when he carved in the evenings, that he woke long before dawn and lay awake holding her when he thought she was asleep, that he liked cod and mushrooms and loathed beets. She knew that he laughed when amused but also to hide uneasiness. Even now, his tense shoulders and jerky movements told her he was still upset about Rorik. Some-how, the impossible had happened—she had learned to live with a man, a husband. And even worse, she loved him.

Gods, she loved him.

His eyes lifted to meet hers. "Why are you looking at me like that?"

She eyed him up and down, admiring his broad warrior shoulders, the rippling ridges of his stomach, and the long thick member that hung heavy between his lean legs.

"Like what?"

She had changed too. And she liked the person she had become around Ivvár. This Edda was not afraid and did not feel like an outsider. This Edda was confident and secure in her place in the clan. And most surprising of all, this Edda wanted to know what it felt like to be truly desired by her husband, even if it meant risking being played for a fool.

"Like I am honey, and you are the bear."

He was not mistaken. She was beyond pretending that he did not look as though he were carved in the image of mighty Thor. Samara had sworn that he'd not taken anyone else to bed since they had been married. Edda had arrived on the island wanting him to satiate his needs elsewhere, but now she was glad he had not. He was hers, and she wanted to know *all* of him.

"Honey is delicious."

His blue eyes heated, grew wild, his cock thickening before her eyes. "Beware, little wife. You play a dangerous game," he said, his voice a low warning growl that made her heart lurch in response.

Sudden darkness settled over the room as he doused the light, and then his warm body slid in beside hers.

Edda rolled to face him, her heart hammering in her chest. She ached to touch him, to feel his hands on her skin.

"Ivvár?"

"Hmm." The shadow of his profile disappeared as he turned his head to look at her.

Edda reached out, her fingers finding hot flesh.

His breath hitched, and she knew he recognized the gravity of this moment—this was the first time she had reached for him, touched him in their bed.

She caressed his arm, her breath quickening with every brush of hard muscle and silky skin beneath her fingertips. She pressed her legs together, turning the insistent ache between her thighs to pleasure. Her hands explored his shoulders and chest, her fingers warming against the heat of his skin.

"Edda…" Ivvár rolled onto his side, wrapped an arm

around her waist, and pulled her closer. His arms surrounded her, the press of his hard chest making her nipples furl into tight buds beneath her thin nightdress. Warm hands sent shivers down her spine as they pushed the fabric up to her waist, baring her sex for him to touch. Just as she knew that the sun would set and the moon would rise, she knew this marriage between her and Ivvár was fated. Her love for him was as steady as her heartbeat. She needed him like she needed air. Whatever that meant for her future as völva, she would accept it as the will of the gods.

Gently coaxing her knees apart, Ivvár moved his legs between hers and guided her thigh up over his waist.

Blessed Freya! All air escaped her as his hard length settled against her womanhood.

She buried her face against his throat.

More. She needed more.

Tipping her head back, Edda pressed her mouth to his and parted her lips, her tongue darting out in tentative strokes.

His response was swift and savage, his mouth demanding in its possession. Unshaven, his beard brushed against her skin as his tongue invaded, tangled with hers, his lips gentle and then devouring—a warrior claiming his prize.

Ivvár kissed her until she was senseless, until her sex rocked in a sensual rhythm against his silky length, and she whimpered her absolute submission.

Her hands roamed down the expanse of his chest, exploring the hard, smooth flesh. The ache between her legs had her rocking faster as her hands dipped lower still. She needed to feel him in her hands, to touch his manhood.

Tearing his lips from hers, Ivvár pulled away, his hand covering hers.

Her lips burned.

She burned.

"Look at me, Edda."

Edda lifted her lids and met his gaze. She could see little more than the shadowed lines of his lips, nose and jawline in the darkness, but his eyes shimmered with emotion.

Doubt doused her raging desire.

Something was wrong.

"Show me your face," he said, his tone demanding.

"Nei." Her voice broke in a pained whisper.

The heat in his eyes cooled, his lips pressing into a determined line. "Rorik hides from me. I will not have that in my marriage too." His fingers trailed down her arm lightly.

Her blood heated.

"I want to love all of you," he whispered, the hoarseness of his voice leaving her in no doubt of his earnestness.

By the gods, she wanted to know what it was to be loved by him. She had never imagined that she would waver from her calling to be völva, but she had changed. Now she wanted Ivvár too, to be married to him, to share her body with him as husband and wife.

"I wore paint in the bathhouse. It seemed not to matter then. I want to love all of you too, like this."

Ivvár laughed and shook his head. "This you cannot control, Edda. I'll not have it. After our wedding, I told you I would not bed you until you gave all of yourself."

Her mind flashed back to that night, her corpse mask, the dagger, his promise.

I swear on the All-father, I will not bed you unless you desire it, until you willingly give all of yourself.

"If you want this…" He motioned between them. "Then you must not hide from me," he said, his tone firm yet laced with pain.

Edda balked. She did not want to hurt him—Rorik had

caused damage enough. Uncertainty made her chest tighten. Did she want to be alone for the rest of her life? Just as a tiny seed planted in dark earth struggled, Ivvár had used the light of his kindness and patience to grow his place in her heart from the barren ground into fledgling affection—and love. His roots were deep now, her passion for him unescapable.

"Take off the mask, Edda." His hands caressed the length of her back gently.

Should she? She winced at the thought of relinquishing the mask that kept a little piece of her safe from the rest of the world.

Ivvár stiffened at her lack of response, the arms he'd wrapped around her falling away. "I will not bed you like this."

His words felt like a blade to the chest. "You will not have me because of the paint?" How could he think she was hiding from him? Just when she had finally let him in, offered herself and even considered baring her face to him.

"I will not. You are *all* I want, Edda, but I shall have all of you or naught. No more hiding."

Desolate misery coiled around her heart, her chest tightening with each agonizing breath. "Keeping the mask on is not me rejecting you, Ivvár. It has naught to do with you."

Ivvár scoffed and rolled onto his back.

He would never believe her. His discord with Rorik kept him from seeing the painful secret she kept hidden—she was terrified of losing him. Ivvár had not spoken it aloud, but she knew he loved her. He had shown her in his actions so often that it was impossible to deny. Yet she knew better than any that love was fickle when confronted with a horrid truth like the one hidden by her mask. Fear clawed at her insides, a violent reminder of what had happened last time.

Pain.

Shame.

Humiliation.

Edda shook her head. She could not do it, not again. She could not cede that last piece of herself to a man. Her teeth pressed into her bottom lip, biting down until the metallic tang of blood filled her mouth and the wound throbbed in tandem with her heartbeat.

An exasperated sigh broke the heavy silence, and the bed creaked as Ivvár rolled over.

Her heart sank as she looked at the shadowy outline of his back in the dim light. The small distance between them suddenly felt like a chasm that could not be crossed.

CHAPTER SEVENTEEN

EDDA

*L*ifting the small square of mirror to her face, Edda ran the brush tip over the bridge of her nose and across her cheek. Her green eyes stared back, a stark contrast to the black kohl she had used on her lower eyelids and smudged in a dark line across her temples.

Strong.

The war paint made her feel powerful, and she needed it after what had happened with Ivvár last eve. Never would she have thought that the husband who had wooed her since they were wed would deny her when she had finally decided to lay with him.

Men!

She couldn't even stay angry with him since even after rejecting her and knowing that he could push for her to yield and bare her face, he had disappeared before dawn to allow her to complete her morning ritual of removing and then reapplying her mask in privacy.

His kindness was relentless. The cursed man wooed her even in his absence.

Jutting her jaw, she firmed her resolve. Too long, she had allowed herself to be his prey, to succumb to his charm. Now she would become the predator, seduce the seducer, and snare him in his own trap.

Painting her mask was usually her gift to herself, yet this time every stroke of paint was intended to attract her husband. Never had she so desperately wanted to know the power a woman felt when lusted after by a man. Long into the night, she had lain awake until she had a plan that she was confident would succeed—she would find ways to lure Ivvár to her, to push him beyond the limits of his restraint until he claimed her.

"Edda?" Ivvár burst into the room, panting.

She shot to her feet and spun around, her heart jumping to her throat. "What is wrong?"

Ivvár's gaze fell to her unpainted lips and cheeks. Heat flared in his riveted gaze before he gathered himself. "Samara is birthing. The babe comes fast."

"Get my bag," she said, turning away to hide her face. For a moment, she looked down at the discarded brush and mirror. She had not yet finished applying the white clay or painting her lips blood red, but Samara needed her.

You can do it.

She swallowed the lump that had formed in her throat. Her eyes were covered, and most of her nose too.

"Do not tarry."

Edda sucked in a fortifying breath when she heard Ivvár move away. Moving across the room to the chest at the end of the bed, she lifted the lid and found her woolen scarf. She wrapped the fabric around her head with deft fingers just as Samara had taught her, leaving only her eyes showing. So long as she was careful, Ivvár would not see her face anymore.

166 | REE THORNTON

"Edda, we must away. They said she is asking for you, and Valen is beside himself with worry."

Power flowed through her fingers and into her body as she lifted her magic staff from where it rested against the wall. Smoothing the skirts on her simple apron dress, she hastened to the door where Ivvár waited.

"Hurry!" He slammed the door behind her, his boots kicking up a cloud of dust as he strode off toward the Jarl's home. "Valen is terrorizing the longhouse."

"Slow down." Edda skidded to a stop at the towering longhouse doors. Her thighs burned from running to keep from falling behind.

Ivvár shook his head. "We cannot. You do not understand. The longhouse will not be left standing if we do not calm my brother's nerves.

"Your brother's nerves?" Edda bent at the waist—one hand pressed to her aching side, cursing men as she struggled to catch her breath. Samara needed her aid, not her entirely hale husband.

The oak doors swung open with a bang, a roar reverberating in the early morning silence. Sleepy-eyed warriors pulled on boots as they streamed through the doorway, followed by women clutching children.

Edda looked at Ivvár and raised a questioning eyebrow. Surely it could not be the Jarl driving his people from the comfort of their beds?

A heavy sigh escaped him. "He is not usually like this, not since Brandr was born."

Men! Edda shook her head. "Warriors have not the nerves for birthing."

Ivvár bristled. "My brother is not a weak man."

Edda approached the doors. "A birthing wife can fell even the strongest of warriors. He must leave, or he will upset

Samara."

Ivvár followed her and handed over her medicine bag. "He will not want to leave her."

"He must. A mother's distress can harm the babe," she insisted as she stepped through the doorway.

The air inside was so heavy that it felt like fog surrounded her, clung to her skin like a spider web, sending shivers up her spine. Waiting for her eyes to adjust, Edda paused and pushed her magic outward, seeking, tasting the mood in the near-empty room.

Darkness.

Despair.

Fear.

Her eyes scanned the expanse of the longhouse where she and Samara often whiled away hours discussing healing. It should have been brightly lit and bustling with the hustle of daily life, but just a few torches burned near the entrance. Huddled near the hearth, three women warmed water in a large cauldron and cast wary looks at the Jarl pacing in front of the doorway to the room he shared with his wife.

Edda turned her attention to Valen, taking in the stricken look on his face. *Foolish man!* The shadow cast by his concern for his wife was suffocating, a black ooze that dripped from the walls and filled one's lungs with every breath.

Dangerous.

Thank the gods that she had arrived before it was too late. Edda hurried toward the Jarl, her boots scuffing on the dirt floor as she crossed the room.

Valen spun around, pinning her with a hard stare. "Where have you been?"

"I am here now."

"Not soon—"

"Quiet!" Edda glared at the Jarl. "You will not birth this babe. Do not speak."

Valen's mouth slammed shut.

Edda watched as the dark cloud surrounding him blurred to gray, then red, spreading outward like a crashing wave.

Good.

Anger could be overcome, unlike the hopelessness of despair. Standing firm against the onslaught of his fury, she pointed to the oldest of the women.

"You... What is your name?"

"Lila."

"Lila, will you see that I have all I need to aid the Jarl's wife?"

"Já, Völva. It would be an honor."

"Very well. Light the torches and have doors kept open. I will need hot water, soap, and many cloths. See to it."

Lila nodded and motioned for her companions to get to work. "Is there naught else, Völva?"

"I have yet to break my fast."

"Bread and cheese? Or I can send for something from the hall?"

"Nei. Bread and cheese will suffice for now." Satisfied, Edda turned back to Samara's husband. "Valen, you and Ivvár will see to the sacrifice for the gods."

The jarl crossed arms wrapped in dark inked designs over his chest, dark blue eyes that were so like her husband's, glowered at her. "I shall stay with my wife," he protested.

"Nei. Birthing is for women, as you well know. I will send for you when her time nears."

His hand caressed his beard as he weighed his options, fear and uncertainty plain on his face.

"All will be well, Jarl. This is not her first babe." Edda patted him on the arm and sent calming energy toward him.

"I will see her through this birthing, and you will both hold your child soon."

Valen's gaze softened at the mention of the new babe, and then he nodded his acquiescence.

"Go now. I must see to her comfort."

"Come, Brother." Ivvár wrapped an arm around Valen's neck and wrestled him to the door playfully. Pausing to look back over his shoulder, he winked at her before disappearing outside.

Edda circled the room three times, her hand tapping in rhythm on her thigh as she chanted. Rushed though it was, her incantation would chase away the lingering darkness. Satisfied that she had done what she could, she hurried toward the bedchamber.

The room was large and filled with a Jarl's comforts—a large bed, a carved table, and two chairs. Colorful tapestries depicting the gods and dyed silks hung from the walls down to the thick furs that covered the floor.

In the corner, Samara stood bent double, moaning.

"I have come, friend." Edda placed her bag on the table, removed her veil, and leaned her staff against the wall. Rustling around in her bag, she pulled some sprigs of mugwort tied together with leather, plucked a few stems from the bunch, and then tossed them on the hearth fire.

Tension eased from her shoulders as she watched the flames crackle to life and the thick purifying smoke fill the space. Her lips moved, chanting to entreat Freya to bless this birth as she drew a small ceramic jar with a wooden lid from her bag and placed it on the table. If the fates were with them, she would not need the Shepherd's Purse tincture renowned for stemming bleeding. Her gaze drifted to where Samara stood.

"You will have another beautiful child soon, Princess,"

Adela whispered the encouragement and rubbed Samara's back. As the woman who had raised Samara and her constant companion, Adela would take the place often reserved for the mother in the birthing ritual.

Edda paused at the sharp pain in her chest. Seeing the two women together, sharing this life-changing moment, reminded her of all she was missing. Her mother had been distant, leaving the raising of her children to thralls in favor of her queenly duties until her death. At just seven summers, she had not felt the loss of the woman that was a stranger to her, and had not known pain until she'd lost Ásta.

A knock sounded at the door.

"Come," Edda said.

The door opened, and Lila entered with freshly torn strands of cloth slung over one shoulder and a bar of soap and bowl of steaming water in her hands. "I have the water and other supplies."

"My thanks, Lila." Edda motioned for them to be placed on the table, grateful when the woman left without another word and softly closed the door behind her.

Edda dipped her hands in the water and began to wash her hands. In the years she had been völva, she had attended many births and witnessed the pain, joy, and even deaths of women bringing life into the world. She knew what to expect.

Droplets fell from her hands as she turned, allowing the composed healer in her to come to the fore. Her focus narrowed to fulfilling her duty—seeing the woman and child safely through this labor before she could step back and disappear into the shadows. This was the way of the völva.

Her eyes met Samara's grey ones and clung to them as a surge of magic closed the distance between them, strong like the ropes used on longships, stretching between her heart and that of her friend.

We are bonded!

The realization left her reeling. This birthing would be the hardest she had ever performed. The bond she shared with Samara would make it impossible to hide her feelings as she had with other birthing women. Her friend would feel the pain she endured each time she helped bring a child into the world and understand that it stemmed from denying herself her one desire, a child of her own.

Edda swallowed hard and squared her shoulders. Come what may, she would not leave her friend to walk this journey alone. She crossed the room and squatted on her haunches, her hands feeling Samara's protruding stomach for the baby's position. Head down. Good.

"Tell me what you feel, friend."

Samara rocked her hips forward and back, her hands clutching at the wooden bed end—a good sign that all was well with mother and child— and then looked down through her outstretched arms. "Brandr did not pain me so."

Edda smiled up at her. "Then she will be a strong girl like her mother."

"The babe comes soon?" Adela groaned, one hand pressing into the curve of her back as she straightened.

"Let's get this baby out, Já? Before Adela needs one of my tinctures for her creaky old bones."

"Who you call old, girl?" Adela shook a finger in her direction, her accent thick and broken when she spoke.

Samara chuckled and then winced before resuming her rocking motion.

"A second birth may be faster." Edda slid her arm around her friend's shoulders, nodding at Adela to do the same. "Come to the bed. I must see how far along you are."

Together, they maneuvered Samara onto the bed, propping her up with pillows.

Edda lowered herself to her knees and began her examination. This babe would come unhindered. She could see it in the relaxed focus of her friend, feel it in the powerful earthly force that connected her, Samara, and Adela in this ancient woman's ritual.

Edda rose from kneeling and nodded at Adela. "The babe will not come before nightfall."

"*La.* It hurts." Samara's head fell back, her eyes closing as her hands gripped her belly through another wave of pain.

"Breathe, Samara." Adela used a cloth to wipe Samara's brow.

Confident Samara was in good hands, Edda moved back to her bag to gather the other items she would need. Iron scissors, a small sharp dagger, and string. Satisfied that she was prepared, she noticed a plate of cheese and bread on the table. Lila must have delivered it and slipped back out into the longhouse unnoticed. Her stomach rumbled in appreciation.

Breaking off a chunk of bread, she took a bite and then nibbled on some cheese. The bread was still warm, the cheese tangy and delicious. As she ate, she watched Adela pull a small ceramic vial from a pouch at her waist.

"Oil," Adela explained in response to her questioning gaze. "Musk. It smells of home."

Edda nodded knowingly. A woman disappeared into herself in the throes of birthing, and an oil that reminded Samara of home and her bond with Adela would make it easier to keep her friend tethered to this world.

Edda finished her meal and washed it down with cold mead. Retrieving her staff from where it rested against the wall, she circled the room and tapped it on the earth in a slow, steady rhythm. Reaching into a pouch tied to her belt, she tossed a handful of dried herbs on the fire. Now the ritual would begin, the offerings, the chants to the goddess Freya. Edda let her eyes drift closed as her lips moved in a low whisper that would increase with each offering given to the fire or earth.

~

$\mathcal{T}$he noisy hustle of life had long given way to the silence of the night when the babe came. Edda walked out of the bedchamber and into the longhouse that was empty but for Lila, the household having bedded down in the Great Hall for the eve.

"Lila! Send for the Jarl." She watched as the young woman shoved the door open and ran out into the night.

Valen would not be far—his brothers had hauled him away three times already this eve, such was his concern for his wife.

Edda moved around the glowing embers of the central hearth and back toward the bedchamber, glad to stretch her legs. Lila had proven herself a worthy assistant, quietly slipping in and out of the bedchamber to provide water, supplies, and sustenance. Her calm nature and gentling presence were rare gifts. If the young woman had any interest in learning the ways of the völva, she would make a promising novice.

Crossing to the bed where Samara lay, Edda nodded at Adela. "Move behind her."

Adela lifted her skirts and moved onto the bed, the weariness disappearing from her countenance now that Samara needed her.

"Valen," Samara moaned.

"He comes," Edda said, lifting Samara's legs and placing them on the floor. "Now, you shall welcome your babe." The birthing would happen with Samara standing braced from behind by the woman that had supported her all her life.

"I am here, Princess." Adela slid her arms beneath Samara's armpits, prepared to hold her aloft through the coming ordeal.

Together they encouraged Samara onto her feet, holding her steady when she swayed.

"It hurts."

"You can do this." Edda knelt between her friend's legs and used a leather strap to tie her skirts up at the sides. After checking that she had all she needed close at hand, she slid her hand beneath the skirts to confirm her suspicions.

"I can feel the head."

Adela nodded, her gaze narrowing to determined focus as she held her Princess firmly. "I be strength when you have none. I be rock when you crumble. We do this together."

A door slammed, followed by pounding footsteps.

"I am here, my love." Valen stepped into the bedchamber, his face wan at the sight of his wife.

Samara's usually silky hair was a mess of damp curls that hung limply to her waist, her skin shimmered with the sheen of sweat, the exhaustion of laboring apparent on her features.

"Come, Valen. It is time to meet your child," Edda said, motioning him closer.

Samara shook her head. "I do not want him to see me like this," she huffed between panting breaths.

Valen crossed the room in three strides and lifted his wife's hand to his lips for a gentle kiss. "Your strength only adds to your beauty, my love."

Edda knelt on a small cushion, her supplies and tools assembled on a small square stool at her side.

A contraction wracked her friend's stomach, the skin tightening so she could see the outline of the baby moving inside. Never had the wonder of life felt so close, so real. Never had the lack of a child of her own bitten so deeply.

Adela slid her hand low, cradling the moving belly, intending to soothe the life within. The older woman had skills known only to those privy to the secrets of birthing chambers. Whatever her life before she had landed on these Viking shores, she had attended many births.

Edda looked up. The time had come to take control. Reaching out, she guided Samara and Valen's hands to the protruding belly and gently rested her hand over theirs.

With a sudden surge, the threads of their magic merged— the four of them and the pulsing light of the new life.

Connected.

A birthing bond!

The babe stilled as the powerful binding magic tethered them together.

All tales of such bonds claimed that they could not form between strangers and thus were unheard of between völva and child. And yet Samara was not a stranger. They were friends, bonded in a way Edda had never been with another woman she had assisted in birthing. And the low hum of the baby's powerful magic called to her like the wind in the trees on a summer day, like the heat of a mid-winter fire.

Irresistible.

Fated.

It made little sense, but who was she to deny the Norns? Somehow, she would play an essential role in this child's journey. Using the connection linking all five of them, Edda sent out a wave of soothing energy that enveloped the room.

"You must push now, Samara."

Her friend's amber eyes opened, her dazed gaze clearing as she nodded.

"Breathe deep and push down. It is time to meet your babe."

Adela held Samara aloft, and Valen muttered soothing words as Samara pushed.

A long squalling cry broke the silence of the coming dawn.

Edda looked down at the plump babe wriggling in her hands as she quickly cut the cord and tied it off. She wiped the child, wrapped it in a blanket, and checked that the babe was hale.

Perfect. Ten perfect fingers and toes.

Edda pushed the blanket away from the baby's face, her fingertips brushing over the softness of its cheek. And then it came—the surge of relief and every other emotion she kept carefully hidden from the world—the painful longing, the deep sadness, and the utter despair that she would never have a child of her own.

"Edda?"

Her eyes lifted to meet amber ones.

Samara held her gaze, her eyes filling with tears as understanding dawned.

Edda shook her head. She may not be able to hide her feelings from her friend anymore, but she did not want her pity. She was no victim. She could have had a child, but instead, she had chosen to become völva, chosen this life and the sacrifices that came with it.

Rising to her feet, she gently placed the baby in its father's waiting arms. "You have a healthy daughter, Jarl Eriksson."

Valen looked down at the child and then at his wife. "A daughter," he said, his voice laced with wonder.

"A girl." Samara smiled tiredly. "May she be strong like her father."

"And fierce like her mother," Valen replied.

Relieved that her friend's attention was elsewhere, Edda returned to caring for the unsightly aspects that followed birthing. Her hands shook as she fought to ignore the painful ache in her chest. Feeling a birthing bond had broken something inside of her, cracked her open. All she had kept hidden, denied even to herself, had been released like a surging crashing wave that could not be contained. Every hope and dream she'd had of the life she had longed for before Ubbe rejected her came rushing back—she wanted a family of her own, to cradle her baby against her chest, Ivvár's baby.

CHAPTER EIGHTEEN

EDDA

The first rays of sunlight broke over the horizon when Edda stepped outside the longhouse and collapsed against the wall. Exhaustion seeped from her bones as the rough timber grazed her shoulder. The birth had taken longer than expected, so she had not long rewrapped her veil and taken her leave from the Jarl's bedchamber.

"Edda?"

"Ivvár," she whispered as she tugged the scarf that hid her face higher.

"All is well?"

"Já. Mother and daughter are healthy." She had slipped from the bedchamber unnoticed by Valen and Samara, who were oblivious to all but each other and their new babe.

Ivvár moved closer, his keen eyes studying her intently. "What ails you?"

Edda turned away. She did not want him to see her like this, exhausted, vulnerable, her barriers almost destroyed. "It is naught. I am weary."

"Look at me." He was so close now that the heat from his body warmed her against the chilled dawn air.

A shiver crept down her spine. He was so rugged, strong, and virile. What need could a man like him have for a woman like her?

"Look at me," he repeated. His voice was more demanding now.

Edda shook her head, keeping her eyes averted and the scarf firmly in place. "Not like this." Not with half her face unpainted and the rest a smudged mess after a long day and night.

"Edda?" His thighs pressed against hers, his hand cupping her chin over the fabric she held fast and then turning her face toward him.

She should have known he would not let it go.

"I am a mess." Resisting the urge to lean into his touch, she pulled away.

"Let me in, little wife."

Edda released a shuddering sigh at his soft, entreating plea. All she wanted was to surrender to him, to his touch, to his body.

For a long moment, his eyes held hers. And when she did not protest, his fingers slid to the edge of her scarf.

Edda knew she should resist, call on the gods and her magic to repel him, but she was too weary for even that poor defense. And without the strength to resist, she was just a woman and he a man, both of them entangled in the bonds of a marriage that tightened with each passing day, bringing them closer and closer together.

Ever so slowly, the fabric slid from her skin as he pulled it gently aside. Her heart hammered in her chest, its every beat reminding her how this man, this Viking warrior, made her feel alive in ways nobody had before.

His thumb softly brushed across her bottom lip, his gaze falling to her bared chin.

Edda froze, her eyes locked on his, everything inside her screaming to run. What would he think? Say? She braced herself for the disgust that was sure to come, for the cutting words that left lasting scars on a woman's spirit.

"I like you like this." The low rumble of his voice was heavy with unmistakable hunger.

"You do?" He liked her pallid and unremarkable skin?

"Já. Your skin glows." The tops of his fingers gently caressed her cheek before he pulled his hand away and stepped back. "I wish I had interrupted you earlier, without the mask."

Her breath caught.

His blue eyes studied her intently. "Being part of such an important moment as a birth must be exhausting?"

Edda shook her head, relieved at the change in the direction of the conversation and the reprieve from his touch. "Not usually, but this time was different."

"Different, how?"

"Völva travel far, so the women we assist are often strangers, but Samara is my friend, and the connection between us made it impossible not to be affected."

"Ah." Ivvár nodded, waiting for her to continue.

"There was a birthing bond. It was both terrifying and…" She shook her head, unable to find the words to explain the overwhelming emotions of that moment, of watching that child take its first breath.

"Perfect." He smiled at her warmly. "I know the awe of watching a seed that you have planted burst from the earth as a seedling, feeling that you are a part of the cycle of life. I imagine it is similar?"

Warmth filled her chest. He understood. "Já. It felt

wonderful." Somehow, Ivvár, with his gentle persistence and ability to see beneath the surface, understood her when she could not find the words. He saw the real Edda.

Yet he did not run. He stepped closer as though he wanted to delve deeper into those places that she kept hidden. Ivvár stayed—he cared—he saw her.

Theirs was a genuine connection, and she could no longer deny it.

"Take me home," she said, linking her arm through his and tugging him along. Now she was faced with an impossible decision. If she followed her own needs and desires, she would risk disappointing the clan that relied on her and losing her place as their healer. Should she stay völva or make a family and a life with this Viking warrior?

* * *

Sitting on the stool in front of her clays and paints, Edda wrapped the leather tie around the hair piled atop her head. The tapestry had been tied back so the hearth fire would light the small bedchamber. After returning home, she washed and saw to her needs whilst Ivvár visited the garden to give Kal instructions for the day.

The remnants of the bonding magic in her veins had now eased to a low hum, and the bed with its rumpled blankets and furs called to her like the goddess Rán beckoned seafarers to their demise.

Söl wrapped himself around her legs, thanking her for the meal she had provided.

As was common in the aftermath of using her power, the exhausted ache in her body had increased since returning home. All she wanted was to curl up under the blankets and fall asleep.

First, she must cover her face.

She had heard Ivvár make his way to the bathhouse not long ago. He would soon join her in their bed for some much-needed rest.

Edda hesitated at seeing all the small glass bottles and pouches lined up in neat rows. Would it be so terrible to let him see her?

No clay. The words echoed in her head. Edda stared at her reflection in the small mirror that rested against the wall. She wanted to try for Ivvár. Lifting the crushed powder, she dabbed it over her face and then used kohl to add a rabbit's black nose and whiskers.

No clay. Would he notice? Edda turned to look over her shoulder as footsteps approached.

Ivvár stepped inside the bedchamber, a drying cloth wrapped around his waist, his bare chest glistening in the firelight. "Are you to bed?"

"Já." Rising to her feet, Edda crossed to the bed and crawled in, her body relaxing into the softness and warmth.

Ivvár doused the lantern, and then she heard the swish of his drying cloth being tossed over the carved wooden bedhead before he settled in beside her.

"It was a long night," he said.

"It is often so." Long but worthwhile. Feeling the birthing bond had made it impossible for her to continue to pretend that she didn't want that for herself. She wanted to be a mother, more than anything, even being völva. Long ago, she had accepted that she would be alone but for the company of her völva sisters, and then she had wed Ivvár and still thought her life as a married woman would be solitary. Instead, she found herself married to an honorable man, a messy and sometimes infuriating man, but a man who offered respect, understanding, and companionship that chased away her loneliness.

In the dim light, she watched Ivvár throw his arm up, and his head fall to the side to rest on it.

"Ivvár?" She nestled in closer, her hand tentatively sliding over his broad chest. Dare she be brave and ask for what she desired?

"Já."

Tilting her chin upward, she looked at Ivvár. Her eyes devoured his handsome features, the angular lines of his jaw, his straight nose, and his full lips. A ripple of anticipation wracked her body.

"Kiss me."

His head turned, and then his mouth covered hers, his tongue sliding across her lips and seeking entrance.

Her blood heated as she allowed him in and surrendered to the gentle command of the hand that cupped her face, guiding the kiss.

His lips and tongue worked in tandem to seduce her, to take the kiss from gentle and coaxing to a desperate frenzied melding of mouths that left her writhing against him.

Ivvár pulled away. In one swift movement, he removed her nightdress and tossed it aside.

Edda shivered as the cool air met her skin, and her nipples furled into tight buds.

"Gods, Edda." Ivvár shifted and then was above her, the hard press of his manhood heavy against her soft flesh.

He settled onto his elbows, his lips seeking out hers once more. Nipping and sucking at her bottom lip, his tongue dipped in and out of her mouth in an enticing dance.

His kiss was…everything. She pulled him down until his chest pressed against hers. She needed to feel him. All of him.

184 | REE THORNTON

And then Ivvár rocked against her, the underside of his sex sliding against hers.

"Oh!" Her back arched, sparks shooting up her spine at the delicious friction.

His hands twined in her hair and cupped the back of her head, his mouth moving in ruthless seduction as his hips thrust faster.

"Look at me," he demanded, breaking the kiss.

Edda gazed up at him through heavy-lidded eyes. "I want it all with you. I want a babe," she admitted, the words escaping before she realized what she had said.

Ivvár froze above her, a throbbing ache between her legs, her only reminder of the delicious ebbing friction denied her.

"You want a child?" he said, looking at her in wonder.

Edda swallowed hard and nodded. "With you, I do."

"Now?"

"Já. Now." Edda kissed him, then pressed her lips to his and gave release to her hunger for him.

He groaned into her mouth, his hips resuming their sensual thrusting as his lips moved with hers, taking, claiming.

Her heart thundered in her chest. He wanted her with an abandon that set her body alight. Soon he would take her, slide inside her to make her his in truth. The fury with which she wanted to be claimed by this Viking, her husband, surprised her.

Emboldened, Edda slid her hand beneath the covers, seeking out his silky steel.

Ivvár released a low throaty moan as her fingers wrapped around his length, the glide of his manhood in her hand becoming unrestrained, wild. He threw his head back, his spine arching as a primal roar left his lips and he released his seed.

Edda gasped at the sensation of his sticky fluid on her fingers, her stomach. He had…

Ivvár collapsed on the bed beside her, panting.

"You…you…" Words escaped her.

His head rolled to the side, his eyes opening to look at her. "Já. I did not mean for that to happen, but when you touched me…" He shrugged, a boyish grin curving his lips. "Sorry."

"Sorry? There will be no babe like…*that*." Reaching for her nightdress, she used it to wipe his seed from her skin before tossing it aside.

Ivvár chuckled and pulled her into his arms, his hand settling on the curve of her bottom. "Nei. There will not, but do not worry, little wife. I can do *that*, all night."

"Show me," she said, her hand dipping beneath the blanket.

His wrist wrapped around hers, halting her progress. "Wait."

"What is it?"

Reaching backward, he pulled his bathing cloth from where he had tossed it over the bedhead earlier and held it out to her. "Show me, my love."

Edda froze, the heated blood in her veins suddenly icy. "I cannot," she said in a hushed whisper. He asked too much of her. She would give him her body, her heart, a babe, but not that, not her face.

"Show me, my love," he repeated, resting his head on one hand and using the other to smudge black kohl from her nose with the cloth.

She recoiled at his firm yet gentle touch. "You know I cannot."

Disappointment darkened his gaze, his lips pursed, and his jaw clenched as annoyance took over. "Then neither can I."

Was he denying her? "But I have only some powder and kohl on my face."

"You still hide from me." He returned the cloth to the bedhead, lay beside her, and released a heavy sigh.

"You are being unfair," she accused, brushing his complaint aside. Now she was glad that she had kept enough of her senses to keep some of the mask on, to protect herself.

Ivvár shook his head. "I think not."

Edda sat up. "Can you not see that I am trying?"

His eyebrows slanted into a frown over eyes filled with sadness. "I see a woman still determined to hide and keep me out."

"Fool!" She stared at him in disbelief. How could he say that? How could he not see that she had gone as far as she was able? "I give you all, Ivvár. I am willing to weaken my powers, mayhap to lose them altogether. Even knowing what that will cost me, I would do that for you. Yet you cannot accept me as I am." Tears pooled in her eyes, and Edda knew they would fall in endless streams down her cheeks if she allowed it.

Pushing back the blanket, Ivvár rose to his feet, seemingly oblivious to his nakedness, and looked down at her. "I asked none of that of you. All I want is for you to be yourself. Be völva if that is what you wish."

"I do."

"And I want you. I want nothing more than to claim you, but not if it means you are sacrificing your dreams and who you are. I would not do that and have you resent me. We can be together and share pleasure without me claiming your body."

Now, after wooing her for months, he did not want her. Her heart sank. What cruel game was he playing with her? "I *want* to join with you. Why do you stop?"

"Gods, Edda!" He threw up his hands. "How can you not see that you and Rorik both push me away, are hiding from me? I will not have it, no more."

The air rushed from her lungs. Ivvár was as hurt by hiding her face as he was by losing Rorik? Hearing it said aloud only added to her guilt and anger.

"I love you," he said softly and reached for her.

Edda swatted his hand away. "You lie. If you loved me, then you would accept the mask. All men are the same—you ask much of women yet give naught of yourselves."

Ivvár yanked on his breeches, and then a deep frown marred his handsome face as he reached for his shirt. "If you cannot see that I give you all of myself, then there is nothing else to be said. It is you who holds back. Why would I want a babe with a woman who hides from me?"

Fury engulfed her with scathing intensity. She had bared her heart to him, revealed the hopes she had denied even to herself for years, and still, she was not enough.

Hideous Edda, hideous, hideous, hideous...

The merciless mantra echoed in her head, reminding her of her worthlessness. She should have never allowed herself to love him. The dangerous combination of tiredness and the feeling of all her hopes slipping away made her lash out.

"It is no wonder Rorik lives as far from you as possible," she said, hitting him where she knew it would hurt most.

Ivvár stilled, his features hardening at her angry retort.

"Get. Out," she demanded.

Ivvár pulled the shirt over his head, tucking it into his breeches as he spoke. "Your mask has naught to do with me or our marriage. What happened to make you like this? What are you truly hiding from? It is not me."

Her lips trembled, panic tightening her chest. "N-nothing."

Ivvár shot her a look of such pity that her stomach clenched.

Her heart thundered, her mind foggy as she desperately sought a way to push him away. Already he saw too much of her.

Ivvár shook his head. "For one with the sight, you are remarkably blind."

Crossing her hands over her chest, Edda leaned back against the pillows and fought to reclaim control of her wayward emotions.

"I know someone hurt you. Do not deny it. I will not have you hide from me."

Her heartbeat refused to slow, her every nerve feeling frayed and on edge. Curse him for doing this to her, for stripping away the lies she hid behind and leaving her raw and vulnerable.

"Everyone else in the clan accepts me like this," she said, disappointed when her words came out haltingly. "They accept the mask."

"I am *not* everyone else, Edda," Ivvár roared. Then his fist pounded against his chest with each word. "I. Am. Your. Husband." Pain flashed in his eyes before he strode across the room with his hands clenched at his sides, the echo of his footstep sounding hollow to her ears.

"Even now, I have given you too much." The anguished whisper escaped her trembling lips as tears rolled down her cheeks.

Ivvár turned and looked back over his shoulder, his blue eyes dark, resolute. "I'll have all of you or naught." His voice was laden with the same vehement promise as a warrior's vow to Óðinn—absolute. And then he left, taking her dying heart with him.

Her aching, tired eyes stung with tears that flowed down her cheeks, no doubt removing the vestiges of the mask he wanted gone—the one thing she could never give him.

CHAPTER NINETEEN

EDDA

*E*dda jumped as heavy pounding sounded on the door three days later. Ivvár would not be returning so soon after their argument, surely? The rooster had barely stopped crowing since she had sent him away when he'd returned at dawn after another night spent with the warriors. His face had remained calm as he'd accepted her ongoing banishment, but she knew better than to underestimate him.

"Stubborn man!"

Of course, he invaded her solitude with that infernal pounding. Ivvár wanted to come back to their home, back into her bed. No doubt, he had returned in another attempt to change her mind. Edda removed the tincture she had been preparing from the fire, placed it on one of the hearthstones, and then hurried to the door.

"I am not feeling apt to forgive you yet…" The words died on her lips as the door swung open. She could not look away.

The woman before her paused, studying her face until recognition dawned. "Edda."

"Ásta?" Edda was too shocked to move, to think.

Ásta's brow furrowed at the sight of the red squirrel mask that Edda had carefully applied that morning, and then their eyes met. "Thank the gods! I was not certain it was you. Sister, I need your help."

Stunned, Edda glanced down at the two small children at her sister's side and then at the babe swaddled in a grey blanket that Ásta held in her arms.

"Edda?"

Edda stared into familiar ice-blue eyes, unable to respond. Her hungry gaze devoured the sight of her sibling. For four summers, she had thought her older sister had died and had mourned her. And then, five winters past, she had received word that Ásta was alive, married, and living in the northlands. In truth, she had not believed it until her father had sent word that his men had confirmed the rumors, for she could not imagine her delicate sister surviving in the harsh winters of the north. But her eyes did not lie. Ásta stood before her alive, although her once admired pale complexion was now ashen and marred by dark shadows beneath her eyes.

"I beg you—my babe is dying. Whatever ill will you hold toward me, please do not turn my child away."

The rattling wheeze of the babe fighting for breath broke the silence between them, and Ásta fretfully tucked the blanket tighter around the bundled child.

Regaining her wits, Edda stepped aside and motioned them inside. "Come warm yourselves by the hearth."

"My thanks," Ásta whispered as she stepped inside and hastened to the hearth.

Edda pushed the door closed and sucked in a fortifying breath. Ásta was alive—in her home. Without even seeing the child, Edda knew it was nearing the veil of death. She had felt the darkness that followed the swaddled bundle as Ásta had passed by her.

A small hand tugged at her skirt.

Turning her head, Edda looked down at a little girl with blond locks braided tight against her head and a smear of dirt across one cheek.

"Who are you?" the child asked.

"I am your aunt, Edda. What is your name?"

"Isá," said the girl.

"I am Jóha," said the boy who came to stand behind his sister.

"Would you like warm pine needle tea, Isá, Jóha?"

Their heads bobbed eagerly.

"Come." Edda crossed to the hearth, tossed pine needles into a pot of water, and placed it over the fire to warm. Leaving the children to watch over the brew, she hurried to Ásta's side.

"What ails the babe?" she asked.

"She cannot breathe. I thought I would have more time to get her to you. Of all the healers, I thought mayhap you could save her, but now I fear it is too late." Ásta's voice cracked as she spoke her greatest fear aloud.

"Give me the child." Kneeling and sitting on her heels, Edda held out her arms. All was not lost. She had seen the child turn toward its mother's voice, the bond between them chasing away the darkness for a few fleeting moments. Naught was stronger than the bond between mother and child. She may be able to use it to pull the child back from the brink of death.

Ásta adjusted the swaddling and gently placed the babe into her arms. "Her name is Káre. She is just three moons, born in mid-winter."

Edda assessed the child's delicate features—her damp

skin was as pale as her mother's, and her lips had a dangerous tinge of blue at the corners. Laying the child on the thick fur, Edda unwrapped the thick blanket.

"Tell me what happened. Were others sick? How long has she been like this?"

"No others have taken ill. On the last moon, she took a turn. At first, I thought it would pass, but I called on the *Noaidi* for healing when her breathing worsened. Naught has worked." Ásta's breath hitched as she choked out the words.

"It is fortunate no others took ill. That means it is not of the water or food."

"I cannot lose her." Ásta's cold hand settled over hers and squeezed, her eyes pleading as she spoke. "If any can heal her, it is you."

A surge of warmth filled Edda. All her life, she had needed her older sister, relied on her for comfort and company until Ásta had wed Njal and moved away. But now Ásta needed *her*, trusting no other to care for her child. For so many years, she had felt less than Ásta, an unwanted responsibility, the plain, discarded younger sister that could never compare to the stunning eldest Sorensen daughter. But that all melted away, faded into insignificance as she looked down at the little babe, her kin.

"It is bad," Edda said as she watched the babe's stomach suck in beneath her tiny ribs with every labored breath.

Ásta began to sob, all pretense of composure crumbling.

Edda placed a hand on her shoulder. "Do not surrender yet, sister. We will fight. I will do all I can to save my niece."

Ásta sucked in a shuddering breath and nodded. Lifting the hem of her dress, she wiped the tears from her cheeks. "Tell me what to do."

"On the bench is pottage. Warm it over the fire and give it to the children. I will care for the little one."

Once Ásta rose to her feet and moved the children to the table, Edda pulled a balm from her medicine bag. It was made from the small purple flowers that grew wild in the meadows, good for fevers and sweating sickness. Dipping two fingers into the infused beeswax balm, she lifted the child's shirt and rubbed it on her tiny chest. As soon as the water boiled, the long day and night of steaming and sweating the illness out of the child would begin, but for now, she could offer comfort.

Tenderly lifting the child, Edda cradled her against her chest and wrapped the blanket around them. Soon, the tiny pitter-patter of the child's heartbeat slowed to match her own, and the babe dozed off.

Letting her eyes drift closed, Edda opened her connection to the gods and began to sing the ancient chants to the healing goddess Eir. Even if it took every breath in her body and all her magic, she would see this child live.

CHAPTER TWENTY

EDDA

*A*s owls returned to hollows and men rose from their beds to face the dawn, Edda sat by the smoldering hearth, looking down at the sleeping babe nestled beside her in the thick furs.

"Is she well?' Ásta's voice was soft yet hopeful.

Edda paused before she spoke. She wanted to offer comfort, yet she would not give false hope or lies. The otherworld was calling to Ásta's child, and it would take all her skill to keep her niece tethered to this world. "She breathes easier. Though I fear it will be a long while before she recovers."

"But she will live?" Her sister's weary eyes stared back at her, awaiting an answer she could not provide. Connected though she was to the gods, matters of life and death were unpredictable, even to the seeress' that foretold events.

"Mayhap if it is the will of the gods. Sleep heals—it is good that she slumbers."

Ásta released a shuddering sigh. "My thanks, Edda. I was relieved when Rúna sent word that you were on Gottland with your husband. Now it feels fated that you can care for Káre."

"You have a lovely family." Edda adjusted the fabric swaddling around her niece. She did not want to think of the husband she had banished from their home under the pretense of caring for the sick babe. The sting of his rejection and their argument had not yet faded.

Ásta glanced at where her older children slept on pallets nearby. "The gods have favored me. I thought I would not wed again after Njal, but Dànel is a good man."

"He could not sail with you?"

"Nei. He wanted to come, but it is the trading season, and his aunt is unwell."

"You are happy?"

A smile lit Ásta's face, reminding Edda of the beauty beneath her sister's weary features. "I love Dànel. We have a good life with his family."

"I am glad to hear it. Tell me of Dànel and your life in the northlands." Leaning over the hearth, Edda pulled a swatch of folded fabric from her belt and used it to lift a small cauldron from the overhanging hook. Holding it aloft, she poured scalding pine needle tea into two drinking bowls and passed one to Ásta. With the sun rising and the children soon to wake, they would need the fortifying brew to get through the long day ahead.

Ásta sipped from the bowl, looking over the rim at her. "Ours was not an easy beginning. I met Dànel in Luleavst. I had been alone since Njal, but Dànel was…very persuasive."

"You were together?"

Ásta smiled to herself as she spoke. "We shared furs one night, but afterward, I felt such guilt that I told him there could be naught between us, and he left soon after. I was carrying his child when I arrived in the northlands the following winter. I needed to hide from Mattias."

Edda swallowed the tea, letting the mild citrusy brew slide down her throat. "Why?" She had never understood why Ásta had disappeared. Njal had died, but Ásta could have continued to live in comfort with her husband's family or returned to their father.

"I saw Mattias give the order for Njal to be murdered. He killed his brother."

Edda felt the color drain from her face. "Mattias planned the ambush?" Surely not? Even the most dishonorable outlaws avoided familicide. "He wanted to rule?"

Ásta nodded. "Rúna helped me escape the ambush and spread rumors of my demise. For years, she gave me a place in her household and hid me when any noble families visited. But then Mattias came to Luleavst and discovered that I was alive. I had to run."

"But Mattias followed you."

Ásta nodded. "He arrived with the winter storms."

Edda set aside her empty bowl. "To kill you?"

Ásta shook her head. "He wanted me for his wife. He was sick in mind, convinced that I was his. He hunted me through the forest like an animal."

"Gods! Dànel must be loath to let you out of sight now." It was hard to imagine her gentle sister enduring such a plight. How had she survived?

Ásta pulled some fabric from a bag beside her, then an iron needle and some thread from a small pouch tied to her belt. "Dànel knows that I am not the fragile, wounded woman that arrived in the Northlands all those years ago. I can protect myself and my children."

Edda waved a hand dismissively, a lump forming in her throat. "I am sorry that I asked you to speak of it."

Ásta shrugged, seemingly not bothered by the discussion. "We cannot undo what is done, only face it and change ourselves." Her head dropped to the needlework in her hands before she continued speaking. "For so long, I was afraid of facing Mattias and living without Njal. My mind held me captive in the past that I could not escape. But there is no place for weakness in the northlands. Only the strong survive. And I had a child to live for."

"What did you do?"

"Dànel taught me the ways of the Sámi. It was exhausting living in the forest—cutting wood, making a fire, erecting the tent. Slowly, I realized I was stronger than I thought and could survive even the harshest snowstorm. And then Mattias found me."

"Gods, Ásta." Edda leaned forward, her finger worrying at the rim of her cup as Ásta spoke.

"I confronted him about murdering Njal," she said, engrossed in threading the needle and knotting the ends.

"You did?" Edda could not picture her gentle sister challenging a Viking warrior to admit his misdeeds, but this woman before her was not the woman she remembered. Ásta still had a waiflike beauty and carried herself with the grace of a queen, yet there was a fire and a hardness in her eyes that warned she was not a woman to be trifled with.

Ásta nodded. "We are the descended of powerful Viking warriors, Edda. To overcome an enemy, we must face him in battle."

"You fought him?" Edda shook her head in disbelief—only a fool would believe that Ásta could outmatch a seasoned warrior at swordplay.

Ásta chuckled. "Nei. I chose the battlefield and faced him. For the first time, I knew my worth. Not a worth determined by a father marrying off a daughter, or because of my husband's power, or even my worth to a clan or kingdom. *My* power, *my* worth as a woman standing alone facing a monster. As I looked into his eyes, I realized I was the stronger of the two of us. I had learned how to survive in the north, and Mattias had not—he was in *my* world. The fear left me before Mattias died. I thought losing Njal had broken me, but even the deepest scars can heal."

Could they?

Edda looked down, shielding her eyes with her lashes. The hurt on Ivvár's face as she'd sent him away flashed in her mind. He cared for her. Could she tell him about Ubbe or explain why it was so hard for her to remove the paint? Ásta had had the fortitude to face down a murderer. Her sister sounded as brave as a shieldmaiden as she told her tale. Could she overcome her past too?

"Enough about me, Sister. When did you become völva?"

Edda looked up, seeing the admiration on her sister's face. She smiled. "It was a little while after you left. I..." Her smile faded as she remembered Ubbe's cruel words. She took a deep breath and said, "I discovered my connection to the gods and was chosen by the priestess Alva to become one of her novices."

"And you paint your face like this?"

Edda stiffened, her arms crossing over her chest. "I am völva," she said.

Tilting her head to one side, Ásta studied her curiously. "You wear it always?"

Edda bristled. She knew what would come next—the request to remove it. Something about the mask seemed to bother those who had known her before. The few times she had seen her father and childhood friends now married with families of their own, they had wanted her to bare her face and see her as she had been when they had known her. Her refusal to do so had never been received well—her father ranting before storming off and her friends' taking offense.

"I do. A squirrel, a fox, warpaint. I wear many faces."

"But not your own?"

"Nei."

"That is a shame. I have missed your lovely face."

Edda shook her head. "Do not speak false, Ásta. Unlike you, I never had the fair face to make men fall at my feet." Regret filled her the moments that the words edged with steel left her lips. It was a foolish mistake to have spoken of her weakness so haphazardly. Ásta would not miss the turmoil that simmered beneath her offhand remark.

"What? You are beautiful." Ásta's brow furrowed, clearly confused at her reaction.

"Do. Not. Lie. I am not a beauty." Edda slung the words like she threw a dagger—hard, fast, and lethal. A sinking feeling settled in her guts. She wanted to crawl into her bed and hide under the covers, not talk about Ubbe and that terrible time in her life, but she had just backed herself into a corner and piqued her sister's curiosity.

Ásta jerked away, her eyes widening in alarm. "It is no lie," she whispered. Her tone was vehement, her voice laced with bitterness when she spoke, "A fair face does not help you to survive, Edda. Beauty comes from within. You've always been beautiful to me, sister. And your face would always be welcome at my door. Yet you hide when most völva do not. Why?"

"That is not what Ubbe said." Edda shifted, pulling her knees up beside her. Her heart hurt as a wave of desolation flooded her body, the same unbearable anguish that had been her existence in her darkest days.

"Ubbe? Ubbe Snorssen? What of him?"

Unable to look at her sister and speak of such things,

Edda looked away. She did not want to share this pain, but
Ásta would not be denied. Biting her lip, she inhaled deeply
and then forced herself to speak. "Ubbe courted me for
months, saying he wanted me for his wife. All along, he had
wanted to win the affections and favor of the beautiful sister
—you."

Ásta opened her mouth, no sound coming out as aston-
ishment touched her face. "Me? We were never…"

Edda sighed heavily, her hands falling to pick at the hem
of her dress. She had known even back then that Ásta was
oblivious to Ubbe. Her heart had belonged to Njal. Yet it did
naught to lessen the pain of Ubbe's betrayal. "I know there
was naught between you, but he used me to get closer to
you."

"He hurt you?"

"He shamed me for believing he would ever want to bed
the lesser sister. He said that not even a princess' dowry
would be enough for a man to overcome his revulsion at my
unsightly face. For years, he and his friends taunted me until
the day I became völva and wore the paint. Then they
feared me."

Understanding dawned on her sister's face. "That is why
you wear the paint and hide your face—to protect yourself."

"I will never be a beauty, but when I wear the paint,
people see that I am völva, powerful."

"Oh, Edda." Ásta's hand settled over her own, warm,
comforting. "They were cruel boys, lying to hurt you. None
of it is truth."

Tears welled in her eyes, threatening to overflow like
when they were younger. "I do not want your pity."

"I do not pity you. I am angry that they would treat you
thus. And now I understand why you resented me. I thought
it was because I would soon marry Njal and leave you

behind. We were the closest of sisters—it hurt when you pushed me away."

"I was unfair. I directed my anger at the wrong person."

"Nei. I should have realized that something was wrong. I was too caught up in my marriage to Njal to see beyond myself."

"You could not have known. I have never spoken of it until now." Some of the hurt and jealousy Edda felt toward Ásta eased. For all her beauty, Ásta's path had been just as difficult and fraught with pain as hers. They had both been at fault for drifting apart. She could have traveled to see Ásta when she had heard she lived, but she had not. Yet the fates had brought them back together to be close once more.

"I am glad you told me what happened with Ubbe, that you trusted me. It helps to talk about our pain." Ásta wrapped her into a tight embrace for a few moments before reluctantly pulling away, smiling. "Does your husband know?"

Edda smiled back. She felt lighter after telling Ásta about Ubbe, but then remembered Ivvár and their argument. Despite being denied many of the benefits of marriage, Ivvár had been naught but patient and thoughtful with her. In truth, she was surprised his frustration had taken so long to boil over.

"You should tell him."

"Let me check on my niece." Rising on her knees, Edda checked on the babe and set another log on the waning embers of the fire before returning to her position across from her sister. Ásta loved her husband and was loved in return. Edda was sure Ásta would never understand the obstacles between her and Ivvár, the impossibility of choosing between her calling or sharing her body and a child with Ivvár. Beautiful Ásta would not understand her fear that if she decided to lay with Ivvár, he would return to seeking out comelier women one day. And even worse, that she would be alone and heartbroken once more, but this time without even her connection to the gods for comfort.

"Edda?"

"Já."

"Will you wear the paint even when you have children? Will they ever see their mother's face?"

Edda stared into the flames, pensive. She'd never considered the repercussions her mask would have on a child as she had never considered a family of her own a possibility. But now it was, and she could not avoid it. Would she hide her face from her child? The thought made her cringe.

'That would be a shame," Ásta said and lifted the fabric from her lap. Her fingers moved swiftly as she mended a hole in the small tunic. "True beauty is strength. And your beauty, little sister, shines brighter than all the stars."

$\sim$

*E*dda sat on a blanket in the garden, her smile joyful as she looked down at her niece. After just five days reunited with Ásta, a lightness had returned to her heart that reminded her of her youth.

Ásta smiled at her fondly. "We will miss your company, Edda."

"As I will miss yours." Now that Káre had overcome the worst of her illness, Ásta and the children would move into an empty cottage nearby until the babe was well enough for the journey home. "I shall visit each morn to check on the little one. Just keep her warm and apply the balm."

"My thanks, Edda. It has been a gift to stay with you."

Ásta looked down at her child, her once pallid features now lit with the soft glow of a mother's love.

"It is no trouble." She spoke true, yet she would be relieved to have some space from the busy demands of three children, and there were others in need of healing that she had turned away these last days.

"Káre is much improved."

Edda ran her fingertips through the soft grass, feeling the buzz of earthly magic joining with her own. "Já. The little one has much to do in this life." She looked down at the naked dozing babe soaking up the sun's healing rays. She recalled the vision that had come to her of this child as a woman destined to heal a great rift. Her life would be a series of battles before she found her true path and fated one.

Now that Ásta and the children were moving into the cottage, Ivvàr would return home from the warrior's quarters. The thought filled her with equal parts of excitement and trepidation. She had missed him, the soft rumble of his laughter, his devastating smile, and the heat of his body wrapped around her at night.

"You offer wise counsel, Sister. Ivvár deserves to know why I wear the paint. I shall tell him of Ubbe."

Joyous laughter from the children wafted on the afternoon breeze.

Edda turned to watch her niece and nephew run through her garden. Returning her gaze to her sister, Edda grimaced. "I have treated you poorly, Ásta. I am sorry."

Ásta shrugged and tilted her face to catch the sunlight. "It is naught."

"Nei. We must speak it."

Ásta looked at her curiously, clearly wondering what would come. "As you wish."

For a moment, Edda paused to collect her thoughts

before continuing. "Watching Johá and Isá play in the garden brings back memories of us."

Ásta glanced at the children. "Já. Children have a way of reminding us of ourselves."

"Parts of ourselves we had forgotten. I had been so caught up feeling abandoned and angry that you let me think you dead rather than trust me with the truth…"

"Oh, Edda! I wanted to tell you, but I needed Mattias to believe it. I could not put you in danger too."

Reaching out, Edda patted her sister's hand comfortingly. "Já. I know that now, but I let my anger cloud all the good memories. Do you remember reciting the tales of the gods as we cuddled under blankets in mid-winter?"

Ásta laughed. "Gods, some of those winters were so cold that my toes went numb when the fire burned out."

"But we had each other for warmth."

"Já. We had each other."

Edda stared at her sister sheepishly. "I am sorry that I forgot all of the good times. You indulged me, even including me in your outings with Njal."

"It was no hardship to spend time with my sister."

Edda's cheeks warmed, her hands coming up to cover her face. "Gods, my fit of temper when I thought you rejected me before your wedding. Ubbe had not long told me he favored you over me, and then you suddenly had no time for me."

"I thought of you often in those years I was hiding from Mattias. It weighed heavy that you thought me dead, but I did not think ill of you once. You were a child, Edda. And you were losing someone you loved."

"A foolish child."

Ásta waved a hand dismissively. "As we all were once, our children will be too."

Edda froze, the truth dawning like a rising sun. Her fear

of rejection came from Ubbe's cruelty when she was a child, but she was a woman now. A woman accepted by her clan, secure in her place as a völva, and content with her life in the bustling village. While a sense of healing had come with that, she would never be free of Ubbe and her past until she faced the scared little girl inside of her that was terribly hurt.

"Let us speak no more of such sorrow. I am glad that Jóha, Isá, and Káre will know their Aunt Edda, the gifted Völva. You must come to visit us in the north."

"I shall. I promise."

CHAPTER TWENTY-ONE

IVVÁR

*L*ost in thought, Ivvár strode along the path that
wound through the forest. He had told Kal that he
needed to collect some wild sorrel to sow in the garden, but
the truth was that he needed to be alone. The quiet embrace
of the trees, the fresh air, and the solitude provided a calming
balm to his troubled mind. He stretched his neck and rolled
his shoulders back. He ached from the uncomfortable nights
spent in an unfamiliar bed while his wife tended to her kin in
their cottage.

"Ivvár?"

Gods! Could he not get a moment of peace? He slowed to
a stop in the middle of the narrow path.

"Seda?" The seiðkonur from Luleavst stood where the
path forked in two, her long carved magic staff in one hand
and her silver tresses fixed atop her head with a leather tie.

"Ivvár," she said in greeting. "I thought it was you."

Ivvár nodded respectfully at the seer renowned for
prophecies that made and destroyed kings. "Well met, Seda.
What brings you to Gottland?" The priestess rarely visited

the island without his brother, Jorvan and his wife, Rúna, the Jarl of Luleavst.

Using her staff to aid her way, the woman approached, her shuffling gait betraying her advancing years. "I travel north to trade with the Sámi."

"Runa and Jorvan too?"

"Nei, they are at Luleavst. Runa carries her third child, another son."

Ivvár nodded. Jorvan often sent word to Valen and the rest of the clan of his growing family. And when the winds favored it, he and Rorik visited Luleavst on their return from the summer raids.

Seda glanced at the gray squirrel scampering into a thicket of hazelnut bushes and then back at him. "I see you escaped death at the *Thing*."

Ivvár grimaced at the reminder of the events that had begun the chaotic upheaval of his life. "Escaped death and gained a bride."

Her beady eyes assessed him thoughtfully. "You are wed?"

Ivvár nodded. "I married one of you." He was surprised that she had not heard of his wedding, given that skalds had rendered his trial and ensuing marriage to King Ake's daughter into song long before he and his bride had even departed the encampment at Uppsala.

Her head tilted to the side, a greying tendril falling across her eye as she looked at him quizzically. "What does that mean?"

"Völva. I married a völva."

The seer looked astonished. "There is a völva on Gotland? Whom?"

Ivvár leaned against the trunk of an oak tree and ran a hand through his hair. "Edda Sorensen, daughter of King Ake."

The tinkle of Seda's laugh wafted on the quiet forest air. "Ahh!" she said knowingly. "This is your punishment given by the King—he has bound you and your family to his own."

Ivvár nodded glumly. "I was foisted with a wife without any of the benefits of marriage."

The seer's brow furrowed. "Of what do you speak?"

"A sword without a sheath," Ivvár said and watched as her confusion deepened. Humiliated that he must speak the words aloud and reveal that his marriage was merely a facade, Ivvár spoke through clenched teeth. "A bee without a flower, woman. I am starving for honey."

The seer's eyes widened as she realized that he spoke of the intimacies of marriage and then confusion once more as it dawned that he spoke of the lack thereof.

Ivvár looked away, his cheeks burning. If he could crawl inside a hole, he would, rather than endure this shame. "You should be laughing. I know you want to." He forced his gaze to meet hers. "I know what you are thinking—Ivvár Eriksson, the renowned skirt-chaser, married to a woman he cannot bed."

At that, Seda did laugh. "What in Helheim do you speak of, man?"

"Bedding a man will weaken Edda's magic. She will lose her connection to the gods. I cannot be the ruin of her calling as völva. I'll not do that to her."

The seeress shook her head in disbelief. "Who speaks such lies? That is not the way of the völva."

"It is not?"

"Nei, you fool. A union between man and woman can yield powerful magic. In some clans, such rituals are used to call for rain or a good harvest."

What in Helheim? A heaviness settled in his stomach. "You are certain? She believes differently."

Seda nodded. "I know it to be true, Ivvár. I have seen it with my own eyes."

Ivvár pushed off the tree and stood tall in the filtered sunlight of the forest as his mind raced. "Then the novices trained under the priestess Alva have been misinformed."

Seda nodded solemnly. "I shall speak with Alva."

Everything Edda had been told was a lie. The guilt that had been weighing on him lifted. He need not fear that seeking pleasure in the marriage bed would steal something from Edda that she cared about deeply and would resent him for later. His temples throbbed as he tried to reconcile it all.

There was naught to keep him and Edda from consummating their marriage.

Except for the mask.

And the argument that had seen him banished from his bed.

He understood Edda's reluctance to let down her defenses when they knew naught of each other, but to continue to hide from him even when they knew each other better had hurt more than he liked to admit.

Seda smiled at him gently. "You should tell her, Ivvár."

"Not yet." A desperate desire to make love to his wife raced through his veins. Yet he would not succumb. She wanted him but refused to trust him. He would not have their first time together be shallow and meaningless. As their bodies joined, he would look upon her face and have Edda know that he loved all of her, every freckle and imperfection. Somehow, he needed to make his wife realize that no matter how she hid her face, she could not hide from what she felt for him, nor him for her. And that those feelings would never forsake them.

"Soon then. She needs to know the truth," Seda said with a pointed stare before walking away.

The truth… Would he ever get the truth? All he wanted was to be close to the people he loved—Edda and Rorik. But all he got in return were secrets. Neither of them trusted him enough to share their pasts. His jaw clenched. Had he failed as a husband and brother? A plan began to form in his mind. He would fight for his wife and marriage until his last breath.

He would not surrender.

CHAPTER TWENTY-TWO

EDDA

*E*dda dipped her head beneath the gnarled branch of an apple tree and walked alongside Ásta and the children toward the Great Hall. She tightened her fingers around her völva staff to steady each footstep. After the birth and the long nights caring for her niece, she was exhausted.

"I am eager for a meal after such hard toil." Ásta lovingly patted the babe cradled against her chest.

"Já," Edda agreed. The waning hours of the day had been busy with moving Ásta and the children into the small cottage and dusting and sweeping in preparation for their stay. "My heart aches to think that we will be parted soon."

Ásta smiled at her fondly. "Me too, Sister."

Edda looked at the sturdy doors of the Great Hall. Her stomach fluttered at the thought of revealing herself to Ivvár. She owed him the truth and owed herself the unburdening of her painful past.

"Hurry, Aunt," Isá said.

Edda looked down as a small hand slid into hers and

tugged her forward impatiently. "It seems we are not the only ones hungry this eve. Let's eat, little one."

Holding her magic staff in one hand and her niece's hand in the other, Edda strode through the doorway and into the Great Hall.

Two long tables filled with clan members and their families lined the sides of the spacious hall. The air was thick with smoke from the hearth and warm from the press of many bodies, all vying for a good meal. Nestled between two wooden pillars carved with renderings of the gods at the back of the room sat Jarl Eriksson and his family. The mood was jovial, filled with the noise of children squealing, men's raucous laughter, and the clatter of trenchers being emptied and refilled.

Isá stumbled to a stop beside her, the little girl's eyes widening as she looked around the room.

Edda smiled down at her with affection. Such a large gathering must seem overwhelming to a child raised in the small community life of a Sami *siida*. Gently squeezing the girl's hand, she urged her niece onward. "Jarl Eriksson serves the most delicious treats in his hall. Would you like some?"

Ásta inhaled sharply.

Edda turned to look at her sister. Something was wrong —Ásta's eyes were wide with shock. Edda followed her gaze. The air rushed from her lungs.

At a table on the far side of the hall, a buxom woman was cuddling up against a familiar red-headed twin with his arm draped over her shoulders.

"Is that your husband?" Ásta whispered.

Her heart refused to believe her eyes—Edda glanced around the crowded hall.

Partially obscured by shadows, she found the Rorik sitting alone and scowling.

Her fingers clenched around her staff. Son of Loki! It *was* Ivvár with another woman.

"We should leave," Ásta said, placing a hand on her shoulder.

"Nei." It felt as though the sun was burning in her chest. She could feel the heat rise through her skin as she strode across the room—molten, fierce heat.

Edda halted in front of the table where Ivvár and the woman were seated. Her staff vibrated beneath her fingers, infusing her with a fortifying power that reminded her she was völva and endowed with the magic of one who touched the realms of the nine worlds. Reminded her she was formidable.

Hushed whispers stretched the length and breadth of the hall, all heads turning toward them in the awkward silence that followed. Waiting. Watching.

"Wife," Ivvár said with a challenge in his eyes and not a hint of shame.

Raising an eyebrow, Edda stared at Ivvár and the woman.

Those seated around the pair hastily rose to their feet and moved away, unwilling to be caught in the middle of a völva's wrath. They expected spells to be cast and curses to fall from her lips. All would be disappointed.

Ivvár looked up at her with a smug smile. Leaning back in his chair nonchalantly, he pulled the woman closer. "This is Ágáta. I can see her face."

Her ire became an inferno. Her power surged, needing to be released and redress the unbalance in her world.

"Who is she?" Ágáta looked confused.

"My wife. Well, we pledged marriage, but..."

Edda watched as Ivvár waved his hand as though she were of little consequence. She would have believed him if not for his eyes, which never left her own, watching closely for her reaction. Her eyes narrowed on Agáta.

"Your wife is völva?" Agáta's voice quivered.

"Leave. Now," Edda said, her barbed and unyielding words shooting across the room accompanied by the force of her magic.

Ágáta's eyes widened as the magic reached her. Keeping her gaze locked on the enemy she had no desire to cross, she shot to her feet and backed away.

Edda pulled her magic back. The woman had made a mistake flirting with a married man, but she was not foolish enough to taunt a völva and risk of finding a cursing pole outside her home.

"You are worse than a rutting goat, husband."

Ivvár rounded the table and approached her. "Are you my doe then, wife?" Seizing her hand, Ivvár tugged her behind him and grabbed a flaming torch from a sconce on the wall, seemingly oblivious to the din of raised voices that followed them out the door. Outside, he walked swiftly, forcing her to run to keep pace as they passed by the garden and then turned down a path leading away from their cottage.

"Where are we going?"

"To the beach." His tone was gruff, annoyed.

"Boots off," Ivvár said. Releasing her hand when they reached the water, he bent to remove his boots and toss them aside.

"Nei." Hands on her hips, she glared at him. She was not a child to be scolded and ordered about, especially not by the husband she had just found with another woman in his arms. He had wronged her, not her him.

Scowling, he stalked toward her. "Now, Edda. Or I shall do it myself."

"Touch me, and I will curse you and your kin forevermore." She wouldn't do that to Samara and the family she had come to care for, but he did not need to know that.

Ivvár shrugged dismissively. "So be it. They are your kin too, Edda. Despite all your protests, you *are* still my wife." With his blue eyes challenging her, he lowered himself onto one knee and lifted her foot.

Edda stomped it back down into the sand with a satisfying crunch.

Again, he lifted it, this time his grip firm and unrelenting.

"Let. Me. Go," she hissed through clenched teeth, her cheeks coloring fiercely.

"Never." He stared up at her, his expression darker than the night sky.

Never. The word reverberated in her head. Was this her fate then, to be wed to a man who did not want her yet would never let her go? Unleashing her frustration, she let her staff fall into the sand and pounded her fists on his back as he pulled one boot from her foot and the other.

Setting them aside, he rose to his feet. "In the water," he demanded, pointing at the shallows.

Edda shook her head defiantly. Why was he behaving like this after shaming her?

Before she could back away, he hoisted her over his shoulder and waded into the small waves.

"Put me down, you oaf."

"As you wish." He swung her off his shoulder and dumped her on her feet.

Her toes dug into the wet sand as she found her balance, the cold water lapping at her knees. She gave him a withering glare. "What is the meaning of this, Ivvár? To make you feel like the big strong warrior carrying off the defenseless women?"

Amusement flickered in his blue eyes. "There is naught defenseless about you."

"Nei. There is not," she agreed.

Their eyes were locked in a battle, neither willing to admit defeat.

"You should go to your other woman. You are not welcome at my door or in my bed."

His shoulders rose and fell as he chuckled. "Agáta is naught to me. I want only you."

"Liar. Why was she in your arms then?"

He waded through the water as he spoke, swiftly closing the distance between them before she could escape. "You are jealous, just as I knew you would be. You love me. Admit it."

"Gods, Ivvár."

"I love you, and I know you love me too."

"What does it matter? I cannot give you what you need."

"You're wrong. A völva does not lose magic when she beds a man." His gaze was sharp, focused.

"Alva said—"

"Alva was wrong," he interrupted. "Seda says that a völva can take a man to her bed without losing her powers, that sex magic can be most powerful."

Edda stumbled back a step. Surely not? Could it be the truth? "I-I *was* taught that it weakens a völva's connection to the gods."

Ivvár shrugged. "There is none more learned than Seda in the ways of Seðir. If she says it is so, then I trust her word." Ivvár reached out. And when she offered no protest, he unwrapped the scarf she had wrapped around her neck before leaving the cottage. "There is no reason for us not to join as man and wife and share the pleasures of the marriage bed."

Bending, he dipped her scarf in the water and held it out.

"Remove the paint, and let me love you. Mask or not, nothing will ever change how we feel for each other. Show me the real you."

Returning her gaze to his, she shook her head.

"No more secrets, Edda."

"I cannot." This was all happening too fast. Everything she believed was being torn away.

Ivvár ran a hand through his hair. "I know you want this too. Have I not been patient, given you time to settle into a new place with a new clan? I offered you all that I am, held naught back."

Edda nodded. "You have."

"Yet still, you shun me. I am a warrior—a man who needs a woman. I deserve to be loved too, Edda. I want that with you. Who you are, the woman I love, does not change when the mask comes off." He was so close now that she could see the pain caused by her rejection in his stormy blue eyes. "What is it that has everyone hiding from me?"

"I will not hide." The words erupted from somewhere deep inside of her.

Ivvár stilled, hope flaring in his eyes.

"I will not hide," Edda repeated, her heart racing at what she was about to do. What he said was true—removing the mask would not change who she was, all she had become. All that would change was that there would be nothing keeping her and Ivvár apart, no secrets between them.

"Truly?"

She grabbed his hand and twined her fingers with his, squeezing gently. "Truly. I am yours, all of me."

Her heart thundered like a herd of wild horses at a full gallop. The moment was here, the one she had dreaded since they had wed, but she would not waver. Her pain was not a burden she wished to share, but Ivvár deserved to know the truth.

Ivvár stared at her as she summoned the courage to speak, his brow furrowing when she licked her parched lips.

Closing her eyes, she inhaled a fortifying breath and steeled herself. It was time to give voice to the pain and leave it behind. Resolute, she opened her eyes and spoke. "I did not want to ever speak of this, but when Ásta shared her story, I realized you needed to know."

"Know what?"

Her stomach roiled, her teeth scraping across her bottom lip. "Th-the paint… You asked me why I would not bare my face to you."

"Já."

She hesitated, unable to choke out the words caught in her throat.

"You can tell me."

Tell him.

Swallowing hard, Edda forced her mouth to move. "When I was four and ten summers, there was a boy."

Ivvár flinched. A slight tick in his jaw was almost imperceptible.

Determined, she forged on before her courage escaped her. "Ubbe was the son of a Jarl that was oath-bound to my father. He had been sent to train with my father's warriors. He-he took a liking to me, courted me."

Everything around them seemed to cease moving. The lapping waves at their knees ebbed to a glassy, shimmering sea that stretched to the moon that hung low on the horizon.

Ivvár remained silent as she continued.

"I was flattered at the attention. You see, Ásta was the beautiful daughter of King Sorensen. No man had ever shown an interest in me before. He was a warrior—strong, powerful, handsome. He was attentive and made me feel beautiful and desired. Before long, he convinced me we would soon wed." Her chest ached as the pain resurfaced. What a fool she had been, childish, innocent.

"What did he do to you? Did he hurt you?" Ivvár asked, his tone revealing thinly veiled anger as his fingers tightened around hers. His hardened expression and the fury in his gaze betrayed the horrors he imagined she had suffered— that she had been raped and brutalized by Ubbe.

Edda placed her hand on his chest. "Oh no, Ivvár! Not that. He did not force himself on me."

His gaze searched hers, the tension easing from his shoulders when satisfied that she spoke true. His thumb brushed across hers, a comforting touch. "What then? Tell me."

"It was the midsummer festival, the same night that Ásta's engagement to Njal was to be announced. All had gathered to feast and celebrate. I had long known that Njal and Ásta would wed. Since childhood, they had loved each other, and it was a good marriage alliance for the two kingdoms. After my father announced the marriage, I went to Ubbe hoping that he would give me my first kiss while my father and his warriors were distracted."

Ivvár covered her hand with his, keeping her palm pressed over the soothing beat of his heart. "Go on."

Her chest tightened, her knees feeling like they would give way as she forged onward to the most painful events. "He was leaning against a table at the far end of the hall, drinking with the other young warriors." Her mind drifted back to that fateful night, her voice disappearing beneath the memories of that fateful eve, beneath the noise of the revelers and the smells of smoke, mutton, and spilled ale as she told her tale.

"May I speak with you, Ubbe?"

"Go away, toad."

The harsh inhale of her breath catching. "What?"

"You heard well. Go away."

The laughter of his friends and the mocking smile that spread across his face as they slapped him on the back.

"But I thought—"

"Thought what?" Ubbe interrupted, rising to his feet and approaching.

Then the press of his large frame against her smaller body, the rough timber of the column he backed her up against scraping across her skin, overwhelming.

"I thought you cared." It was barely a whisper—one she had not realized had escaped.

"I care more for the dirt on my boots than you, little girl." His sneer was ugly, cruel. "You were a game, Edda, merely a ploy to get closer to your sister. Ásta is the one I wanted."

"Ásta?"

"Já. Never would I bed an unsightly toad such as you. Not even all your father's gold will be enough to buy a husband for the daughter with a hideous face." Words that crushed her worth with devastating absoluteness.

Broke her.

"What in Helheim?"

Ivvár's roar shattered the painful haze of her memories, and she was back standing in the frigid water, tears rolling down her cheeks.

"Who is this cur? Ubbe from whence?"

The hand that held hers against his chest fell away, leaving her feeling bereft. Edda knew that expression Ivvár wore—that of a man bent on vengeance. Her heart felt like it would burst through her chest. She wanted to leap into his arms and kiss him soundly for wanting to defend her, but she would not encourage him. Ubbe had stolen too much from her, and she would allow him no more intrusion in her life or marriage.

"Who are his kin?" Ivvár demanded.

Edda shook her head slowly. "He matters not." She slid her hand up his chest to the nape of his neck, stroking his hair. "I want no vengeance, only you."

Ivvár stared down at her, the anger slowly subsiding from his gaze as a new understanding passed between them. "Is this why you hide your face? Is it he that has kept you from me, not because you wanted to be völva?"

"It is both. I... After what happened that night, Ubbe and his friends taunted me with cruel names whenever they cornered me alone. Eventually, I believed that none would want me, so I became völva and gave up on my dream of having a family and being a mother. I devoted my life to healing the ill and my connection to the gods. That was all I wanted...until you."

Ivvár wrapped an arm around her waist and pulled her firmly against him. "You want me?" His voice was tender, hopeful.

With a shy smile, Edda nodded. "I am weary of living like this, hiding. I want to be me. And I want you."

His blue eyes held her captive, smoldering with a sensual promise that sent a delicious warm shiver through her body. "I don't care about the mask, Edda. All I want is you." Ivvár slid his hand into hers, the rough brush of his palm against hers comforting as he led her back to the beach. Crouching on his haunches, he lifted her foot, brushed it off, and shoved it in her boot.

'What are you doing?"

Lifting her other foot, he did the same. "Taking you home, little wife."

CHAPTER TWENTY-THREE

IVVÁR

*I*vvár secured the door and watched Edda bend over to tug at her laces and kick off her boots. His manhood stiffened at the sight of the curve of her hips and the firm globes of her bottom. He had never wanted a woman more. Thank the gods that he need not hold back any longer.

Straightening, she turned to face him, the yearning in her eyes calling him to her.

Ivvár opened his mouth.

She pressed a finger to his lips to silence him, then stumbled over her words in her haste to get them out. "I want to say that... I-I know that I am not the beautiful wife you may have chosen for yourself, but mayhap one day you will desire me as I do you."

Her finger fell away, and she took a step back.

"Edda..." His ire rose at the cowards that had made her think she was not beautiful. How could she believe that he did not desire her? Each night, he thought of only her as he pleasured himself in the bathhouse in a futile attempt to

224 | REE THORNTON

control the urge to claim her body and quench the yearning to feel her quiver around him. Yet still, he craved her. He knew now that naught would sate his desire for her but to lose himself between her thighs.

Edda turned away, her hands trembling.

"Look at me, Edda."

She shook her head and started to turn away.

Ivvár cupped her chin and gently turned her head to face him. The uncertainty in her gaze only added to his resolve. Enveloping her tiny body in his, he pressed her face to his chest. His body hummed. He would not let her avoid him, not after all she had revealed.

Not ever.

"Ivvár?"

"You will not hide from this, from me." Determined, he stepped forward, his leg between hers, guiding her backward.

Her breath caught as she hit the wall. Avoiding his gaze, she wet her lips with the tip of her tongue.

"You are a brave kitten." He leaned closer, his cock hardening as he felt the furled buds of her nipples pressed against him.

Her eyes lifted, and the hope he saw in them almost destroyed him.

"You were little more than a child when you were used and wounded by the very worst of men." He struggled to keep the anger from his voice.

Edda shrugged. "It is not an uncommon story—a woman wounded by cruel tongues."

Nei. It was not, but he would not let her belittle the pain inflicted on her. "Do not dismiss the wrongs done to you, nor your strength. When others would have been defeated, you fought back. You created a new life for yourself and

became a gifted healer." She could not deny herself that
victory.

Edda lifted her chin and stood a little taller. "Já." Her tone
was still wary. "Yet still, I am broken."

Lowering his head, Ivvár brushed his lips softly over hers
in a gentle kiss. "We are all broken, Edda. It is our scars that
strengthen us. The rift between Rorik and I grows with each
passing year—the loss is agonizing. It is a scar I will bear
until death."

"I am sorry, Ivvár."

"As am I. But that is Rorik's fight now, not mine. After
Lasse died, I swore never to become attached to another. I
spent the summers at sea, fighting and voyaging. I stayed
away from my family, clan, and the painful memories that I
knew awaited me here. And then there were the women…"
Ashamed, he looked away and ran his hand through his hair,
unsure how to explain.

"You bedded many so you would not become attached to
one," she mused aloud, and then as understanding dawned,
her features softened.

"And then I met you…"

"Me?" Her brow furrowed in confusion.

"Já. I find myself very attached to you, little wife."

"You do?" Edda shook her head. "But you will not
bed me."

"I want to love your body…" He gave her his best seductive smile and then bent and whispered in her ear. "Very,
very, thoroughly."

He smiled to himself when her breath caught and her
body swayed toward him. Seducing his wife would be most
enjoyable, but first, there were misunderstandings to resolve.

"You believed in giving your body you would lose your
magic. Healing makes you happy, Edda. You would have

resented me for stealing your purpose from you. I could not risk losing our bond, losing you. I can live without pleasure, but not without you."

Her auburn hair glimmered in the firelight as she shook her head. She did not believe him.

Cupping her chin in his hands, Ivvár stared into her eyes, allowing her to see the truth reflected in his. He bared himself to her. "There has been no other woman since we wed."

"None?" Her whisper was soft, hopeful.

"None, little wife. You are the one and only. When we are apart, my thoughts are of you, of your smile, your laugh, of coming home to you. I am yours."

"You do not want a beautiful wife?"

Pulling her into his arms, Ivvár silently vowed that his new purpose would be to dispel every doubt she had about her beauty and worth from her mind. "I have a wife of such beauty that the gods would fight just to walk in her shadow."

She brought her hand up to stifle her laugh. "You *do* love me."

Their eyes locked, their breathing fluttering in unison.

His fingers twirled in a strand of her hair before tucking it behind her ear. "With all my heart."

* * *

Edda lifted the cloth from the murky water and twisted the fabric. Cool liquid ran between her fingers and trickled off her hand, sending ripples through her reflection on the smooth surface of the washbowl.

Her bared face.

She pressed the damp cloth on her forehead, cheeks, and chin, relishing the coolness as she wiped the last of the clay from her face. Fresh night air caressed her bare skin, chasing away the burden of years of heartache.

A heavy shuddering breath escaped her.

Ivvár's hands settled on her shoulders. "Are you well?"

She remained facing away from him.

When she did not reply, he squeezed her shoulders gently and continued. "You do not need to do this, Edda."

"I must," she said with a steely strength forged in pain. She lifted her head and straightened her shoulders. There was no denying that the pain of Ubbe's rejection and a childhood overshadowed by Ásta had been the spark that pushed her on the path to völva. Yet she had earned the respect of her sisters and her place as a teacher to novices, not by being a daughter or wife of a King, but of her own accord. Removing the paint would not change that. She was a völva because she had devoted herself to her calling, and nobody could take that from her, ever.

Edda smiled at the freedom that knowledge brought. It was time to be as brave with her heart as she had been in following her calling, to trust the man who had proven himself worthy. Without another thought, she turned on her heel and faced Ivvár.

Heat flared in his gaze. His blue eyes clung to hers, speaking to her, telling her he did not need to see her face to be sure of his heart.

The air between them thickened. And with heart-pounding certainty, Edda knew that mask or not, Ivvár loved her.

His hand rose to cup her chin. Gently, he turned her face one way and then the other. "You are breathtaking."

Edda leaned into his touch and pressed her cheek against his warm palm. That he thought so was all that mattered.

His thumb slid across her cheek, his calloused touch

reminding her that he was a warrior, a protector. And that, unlike in her work healing the ill, she did not need to be strong with him.

"You needn't say that."

"I would not lie to you, Edda. You. Are. Beautiful," he said in a low, seductive growl.

A delicious shiver crept down her spine as heat pooled between her thighs.

"Even if I'd had the choice, I would choose you a thousand times over."

Edda looked up at her husband, the Viking warrior, a man with dirt under his nails, connected to the earth and the magic of all life. With him, she felt safe, heard, and cherished.

Mine.

"Kiss me," she whispered, pressing her body against his.

His head dipped, his lips grazing hers.

Her lips parted, her tongue darting out to meet his brazenly. Rising on her toes, she kissed him boldly, sliding one arm around his neck as the other tangled in his hair.

Heat coursed through her body as she felt the magic in their bond hum and twine them together.

More.

Ivvár broke away.

Her chest heaved as the room returned to focus.

"Edda." Her name was a plea on his lips as his mouth left a trail of hot kisses down her neck.

Edda slid her hands across his broad shoulders and then down the taut muscles of his arms. Her body felt heavy, warm. She needed this, him. To be loved by the man she loved.

"Take me to bed, husband. I would know all of you."

Sweeping her into his arms, Ivvár crossed to their

bedchamber in three strides and lowered her to her feet. Slowly, as though unwrapping a precious gift, he lifted her dress and then her nightdress over her head and cast them aside.

Resisting the urge to cover herself, Edda stood, waiting. She would not hide from this man she loved, never again.

Her pulse quickened as his smoldering gaze raked downward. And then she was on the bed, and he was coming down atop her. His hard flesh against her soft, sending a shiver of delight down to her toes.

"You." His tongue darted out, tantalizingly soft as it slid across her lips.

"Are." His head dipped, his warm mouth enveloping her nipple, suckling and biting with ravenous fervor.

Edda moaned at the sudden pulsing between her legs. Her blood heated as she lost herself to his sensual caresses as he ravished her, everywhere.

"Beautiful." He moved lower, his mouth trailing across her stomach.

And then he was *there*.

Her hand fell to his head, tangled in his hair.

Lifting his face, he stared up at her, his expression questioning. "I want to taste you."

Unable to resist the earnestness in his eyes, she nodded her surrender and sunk back onto the bed. Edda closed her eyes, her every sense flaring in awareness. Warm furs caressed with skin as the loudness of his breath filled the quiet room, and the heat of his fingers slid over her sex, parting her.

A whimper escaped.

His thumb swept over her nub of bundled nerves, teasing until she ached with need.

Blessed Freya!

Her back arched as his mouth pressed against her sex, licked, sucked, devoured her.

His hands settled over her breasts, plucking and teasing at her nipples. His every touch urged her higher and higher, sending sparks shooting up her spine. She was so close that she could feel the veil between the otherworlds.

And then he was gone.

"Nei." Her eyes opened.

Ivvár held himself above her, a satisfied grin on his face. "You are delicious, little wife."

A hot flush warmed her cheeks, and she shoved his chest half-heartedly.

His eyes twinkled as he chuckled. He lowered himself over her, his manhood pressing against her slick core.

Her blood heated.

"Do you wish me to stop?" he said, his voice earnest.

Edda writhed beneath him, throbbing where his manhood pressed against her.

"Look at me, Edda."

Her eyes met his, their bond pulsing in the air around them.

"I want this. I want you, Ivvár."

He brushed a damp hair from her face and pressed his lips to hers. His mouth moved to her neck, trailing upward until his breath caressed her ear.

Edda shuddered, not wanting to speak—or move—lest he stop.

His teeth scraped over her earlobe, his tongue teasing and sucking on her soft flesh.

"I am yours," he said, his low growl a promise that stole the air from her lungs. Before she could recover her wits to respond, he thrust, impaling her.

Edda froze. There was a moment of pain, then unfamiliar sensations that swelled to overwhelm her.

"Breathe, love." Ivvár held himself still while his mouth sought hers.

Running her hands through his hair, she clasped him close as they kissed, her hunger matching his own. Enveloped in his body and with his mouth allowing no reprieve, his slow coaxing kisses eased the tension from her body. He tasted sweet, like honey mead, and the undeniably alluring flavor of a primal warrior.

Her body tingled and ached with need as he lit a hunger inside her. She felt the warmth where his chest pressed against her breasts, every brush of his lips as they trailed down to the hollow of her neck, the delicious tension of his hands in her hair.

Clenching his jaw, Ivvár slowly rocked his hips, the slow sensual glide of his silky steel wrenching a tormented moan from her throat.

Strange sensations flooded her body. *What was this magic?*

Then he moved again, and Edda lost all coherent thought, surrendering to the primal rhythm of flesh meeting flesh.

"Gods, Edda," Ivvár growled.

And then she knew he felt it too—the invisible, twining, pulsing magic that flowed between them and anchored them to each other as they moved as one. To the very core of her being, she knew that it was an ancient, earthly magic that couples had shared from the beginning of time, the eternal thread that was life and bore life all at the same time.

And then she saw it—the rainbow bridge, shimmering as it stretched toward Asgard—calling to her. Her lips parted, a keening moan escaping as she soared.

Ivvár groaned in her ear and joined her.

With the powerful magic of their joining reaching

outward, Edda felt connected to the earth, the gods, to everything. She saw what was, and all that would be, in the infinite stretch of lifetimes to come. And she knew the truth, the part she was to play in the future of this island, this clan.

Völva.

Lost in the pleasure of their coupling and the images that flashed through her mind, she knew the powerful healer she would be until her end days. Sharing her body with Ivvár did not steal her ability to connect to the gods.

Nei. The purity of their love for each other, of their bodies joined in love, brought its own power.

Muscles fatigued from their lovemaking, Edda snuggled into the crook of his arm and sighed in satisfaction. She had seen the future with absolute clarity— in this lifetime she would have it all—Ivvár, family, and her calling to be völva. Closing her eyes, she let sleep take her.

CHAPTER TWENTY-FOUR

IVVÁR

*I*vvár leaned back in his chair and sipped his ale, eyes scanning the Great Hall. It had been a subdued meal with the men weary from the long day working the fields in the harsh sun. All the young families had returned to their beds long ago, and now just a few warriors and latecomers remained.

Searching the room, he found Edda sitting at a table chatting happily with Ásta. He smiled at the memory of his bride's joyous cries of pleasure, of her insatiable appetite. A full moon had passed since the night they had first joined, endless nights of learning about each other's bodies and finding satisfaction together. Just the thought of their love-making had his cock thickening and his balls aching with need. The Norns could not have fated a more perfect woman for him.

Adjusting himself, his attention shifted to Edda's sister. Ásta's babe had long recovered, yet she still delayed her return to the northlands to remain close to her younger sibling. He was glad for it. Edda had needed this time with

Ásta to forgive herself for how she had treated her kin and heal the rift between them.

"Your wife is happy?" Rorik asked as he lowered himself into a chair.

"Já. She is content." Satisfaction filled him as he thought of how far they had come since that first night they had laid together. Now they shared all—their hopes, dreams, and the shadows of guilt and fear that haunted them. And with the turning of this last moon, Edda had stopped wearing her paint altogether, and he'd known she had finally laid her past to rest. He adored the strong lines of her angular jaw, her sandy-colored complexion with a smattering of freckles across the bridge of her prominent nose that brought her features together. The first day she had ventured outside unpainted, his heart had warmed seeing her smiling with the radiance of the summer sun, her face no longer hidden behind her mask.

"I am glad for it."

Ivvár turned to look at Rorik. His twin had been avoiding him since their argument in the garden. He'd never wanted to hurt Rorik, but he could not regret his words. He would no longer chase the brother that shut him out, nor make excuses for his absence from clan life. Rorik must walk his path alone now, answer for his actions, and mayhap someday find peace and return to the clan.

Rorik avoided his gaze. "I feel your light more too."

Ivvár resisted the urge to sigh. Stubborn and foolish though Rorik was, they were twin souls, and he could not bring himself to feign coldness with his other half. "Já. I am happy, brother. Did you see the garden? I finished two days ago."

"I have not." Rorik twisted his cup in his hands, looking over the rim at him.

"I dreamed of Lasse last night." In the past, he had rarely spoken of his mentor with his brother, not wanting to talk of his friendship with Lasse lest Rorik feel cheated in having a mentor he loathed. But he had resolved to stop shying away from speaking the truth to his twin—Rorik was not a child that needed protection.

"Edda says the dead visit for a reason. In the dream, Lasse reminded me that we all put down roots that spread, nourish, and feed ourselves and those around us. I thought he was lost to me when he died, but I was wrong. Lasse is in the trees, the leaves, in the very earth he nurtured. Whilst the garden lives, he lives too."

Rorik studied him thoughtfully. "That pleases you?"

"It does. And now that I am married to Edda, I will send roots into the earth and have a family. I will work in the garden and pass along the lessons Lasse taught to Kal."

Rorik looked at him dubiously. "You enjoyed being in the garden with Lasse?"

Ivvár pushed on, determined to ignore the discomfort of his brother. "Since I can remember, the garden made me happy, but I never wanted to be, never allowed myself to be."

Rorik jerked back, his shock evident.

He should have explained this to Rorik years ago. "I knew you were unhappy with the herder, loathed killing the animals. It felt unfair to have joy when you could not."

A shadow crossed his brother's features, uneasiness and disquieting truth falling like an ax between them. Awkwardly, Rorik cleared his throat. "One of us should be content in this life. I want you to be contented."

"One cannot live with Edda and not feel joy. I am more than pleased with my life. You could find happiness too, Brother."

Rorik looked thoughtful, as though considering the possibility.

Encouraged, Ivvár continued. "Sometimes, when you plant a seed, you do not get what you planned, and then it grows into a mess of overgrown weeds you need to remove."

"You speak riddles."

"I should not have said that you would be alone forever. I was frustrated. I know that something happened to make you shut me out, to push everyone away. Mayhap it has to do with Gilda's disappearance, mayhap not." Ivvár shrugged and stared into eyes identical to his own. "Even if you never tell me, I will never abandon you."

Rorik shook his head. "I'll never be rid of you?" He said it with an annoyed huff, but Ivvár could hear the relief in his voice.

"Nei, brother. Even in death, we shall sit shoulder to shoulder and feast in the hall of Valhalla."

Rorik punched him in the arm, then abruptly turned away and drained his cup.

Ivvár quietly exhaled. Small though the gesture was, he knew it was Rorik's way of saying that all was well between them.

Rorik placed his cup on the table and motioned at where Edda sat with Ásta. "You'll not be fighting this summer? There is talk of war, and Valen has been asked to send men."

"Nei. I have much to do here." Ivvár raised an eyebrow at his brother, his question unspoken.

"I will fight. I need to go."

Pursing his lips, Ivvár shook his head at his brother's foolishness—the man was more stubborn than a mule. "It won't work, you know."

"What?" And, with the return of that gruff tone, any sense of brotherhood between them was gone.

Bemused, Ivvár leaned back in his chair and watched his twin rise to his feet and round the table. "Hiding from the world and cutting yourself off from people so you don't get hurt. Someday a woman will pull your heart out of your chest and claim it. There will be naught you can do to stop it."

"I live in a hut in the forest..." Rorik tossed parting words over his shoulder as he strode toward the door. "She'll have to find me first."

CHAPTER TWENTY-FIVE

EDDA

*E*dda stood naked but for the flower wreath that adorned her head. The moonlight kissed her skin, invigorating the runes she had painted on her body. Beyond the orchard, the bonfires of the summer solstice celebration burned beneath a full moon. The night was quiet, but for the hoot of an owl hunting over the distant fields, the earlier revelry of the clan having waned as many stumbled to their beds.

"Edda?"

She turned to see Ivvár coming toward her, bending his head to pass beneath the branches of the apple and pear trees. She couldn't look away.

Clad in his pants and boots with his sword hanging at his waist, Ivvár moved with the confidence of a man sure of himself and his path in life. Bare-chested, he glowed in the moonlight, his powerful stride and toned muscles giving him the look of a Viking warrior come to capture his bride.

Her blood heated. Capture her he had, entirely. Unexpected though her marriage had been, she had no regrets about that fateful day they had met at the *Thing* and all that had followed. The fates had chosen well. Ivvár, with his earthiness, was the perfect balance to protect and ground her when she fell under the spell of the often untethered and heady power that came with being völva. Alva had not been so blessed and had abused her power by withholding knowledge to control the novices that looked to her for guidance. Now that the sting of that betrayal had faded and she knew Seda journeyed to the novice village to rectify the wrongs done, Edda felt only pity for the woman she had once considered a dear friend.

Ivvár slid his gaze over her person and lingered on those places he loved most before lifting to meet hers. "Little wife?"

His hungry growl reverberated through her body. She smiled as he stopped before her, eyes blazing with fervent promise. "Husband, I would have us make the midsummer offering as one."

Tilting his head, he looked at her questioningly. "As one?"

Though they both knew that he understood her intent, she gave the explanation he sought. "You know I spoke with Seda before she returned to Luleavst?"

"Já." He folded his arms across his chest, purposely giving her a view of his sun-bronzed muscular arms. The man knew exactly how to tempt her.

As she did him.

"Seda spoke of the joining ritual magic." She bent to slowly retrieve the wooden bowl and brush from the smooth stone she had set them on earlier. A throaty laugh escaped her when Ivvár groaned at the sight of her rounded behind and glistening sex. "She revealed all that Alva hid from me," she said as she straightened.

"What of it, wife?" This time, his growl was deeper, dangerous.

Edda grinned, licking her lips slowly as he watched with an intensity that made heat pool between her thighs. "I would have us do the ritual together this eve and share our magic with the earth as so many have before us."

His eyes widened in disbelief. "You would take me here?" He looked around the silent orchard, down at the smoldering fire and the blankets she had laid on the ground. "Under the moon?"

"Já. Unless you are afraid to be seen, husband?" she teased.

Heat flared in his eyes in answer.

A smile tugging at the corner of her lips, Edda dipped the brush into the plum-stained clay paint, pressed it to his chest, and began drawing the runes.

Ansuz for prosperity.

Berkanan for growth.

Tiwaz for victory and honor.

Jera for a fruitful harvest.

His nipples hardened as the brush swirled over his skin, another throaty groan leaving his lips.

She loved that she could do that to him, make him yearn for her, bring this strong warrior pleasure. Her hand slid down over the hard length tenting his pants and then back up to the tie holding them in place. A tug later, the pants fell. He stepped out of them, his gaze darkening as she dropped to her knees.

"Gods, Edda." His cock jumped.

She smiled up at him brazenly. She knew what he wanted, what he thought she would do—take him in her mouth and pleasure him. Not this time. Lifting the brush, she resumed painting the symbols across his powerful thigh.

Ivvár gave a frustrated grunt, his hands delving into her

hair from the base of her neck upward and then pulling gently.

Her head moved back, her lashes lowering as she reveled in the delicious tension on her scalp.

"Naughty. Teasing. Wife."

Amusement lit his eyes, and she laughed.

"I want to kiss you," he said when she had completed her task and set the bowl and brush aside.

Grabbing his hand, she rose to her feet and led him to the blankets. Pausing, she threw a handful of henbane on the embers of the fire. As sparks flew up toward the starry sky, her eyes caught and held his as she recited the chant Seda had taught her that would enhance the herb's power.

Ivvár stood patiently, his hand clasped with hers, eyes locked on her. She could feel his desire for her rise with each word she uttered, and that seeing her embrace the part of her that was völva only made him want her even more.

Heart racing, she lowered herself onto the blankets and pulled him down.

Ivvár settled between her thighs, his hard length between them as he relinquished all pretense of control and took her mouth in a searing kiss. He offered no mercy—invading, plundering, and conquering her senses.

Her hands cupped his jaw, her ardor matching his as she kissed him back. Their magic hummed in rhythmic waves, shades of blue stretching out and twining together in a rope as solid and unbreakable as the passage of time. *Gods!* She needed him, ached to feel that bliss when he sheathed himself within her.

Attuned to her needs, Ivvár claimed her with one sensual thrust of his hips.

Wrenching her lips from his, Edda threw her hand over her head and dug her fingers into the earth. "Move," she pleaded. Calloused palms covered her hands, her breath catching as his fingers slid between hers and into the earth.

"Perfect." The whisper fell from her lips like a reverie. Somehow, Ivvár knew the ritual's power would be amplified by touching the ground together.

"Mine," Ivvár said, his breath hot against her ear. And then, in a perfectly synchronized dance, his hips began to move, each thrust matching the rhythmic pulsating magic of the earth.

"Já. I am yours," she replied before surrendering entirely to the rising tide of their shared pleasure. She felt the apple trees pulling nourishment from the earth and sending it to the leaves at the farthest edges of their branches, heard the cries of owls soaring overhead, the wolves howling in the distance, and even the bees humming as they joined the joyous cadence of life.

Their bodies were slick with sweat when Ivvár bucked above her, the tendons in his neck taut as he threw his head back and roared his release.

Her back arched, her mouth falling open in a silent scream. She felt the magic of the earth and their own combine like a lightning bolt—power flowed like molten steel through her fingers, filled her, spread outward, and enveloped the land far beyond the planted fields.

Edda soared, awash in a flood of bliss and his potent, virile scent. And the vibration of their magic spread like a mist across the land, becoming one with the earth that would sustain future generations.

EPILOGUE

IVVÀR

*W*ind, so cold that it made his fingers ache, shook the highest branches of the trees overhead. Ivvár looked across the garden at Edda. He should have insisted she stay inside now that the icy winds that heralded winter had arrived. Not that she would have listened. His wife delighted in thwarting his attempts to protect her and their unborn child.

Wrapped in thick furs, Edda sat on the long bench he had placed in the village garden so she could meet with those needing healing. Dressed in a hood and gloves the shade of wild strawberries and lined in lynx fur, and with kohl-darkened eyes and three yellow lines painted down one cheek, she looked like the powerful völva lauded in the poems of traveling skálds.

Mine.

Warmth coiled around his heart like a warm embrace. As the last rays of the sun disappeared beneath the horizon each day, he thanked the gods for bringing Edda to him. She was his, but he gladly shared her with those in need, carrying her bags or escorting her on horseback when she was needed at another village on the island. He was proud of all she did for his clan. He only wished she would not work so hard, especially not in her condition.

Beside Edda sat the widow Sefa and her son Gorm who still cradled his healed arm against his chest. Many moons had passed since the boy had fallen from the tree, and he was long healed, but Edda said that Gorm now suffered an affliction of the mind and feared using the arm he had broken.

Sefa listened attentively to his wife, nodding in-between shooting troubled looks at her loudly protesting son. His was a cure that Edda had known would not be well received. Yet she was adamant that Gorm must resume using the arm or risk enduring a much longer recovery.

Ivvár studied his wife for any signs of discomfort, but she appeared content sitting outside in the cold, tending to those in need of her healing.

Söl nudged his leg and purred for his attention. The feline had softened toward him remarkably with the changes between him and Edda until the cat's relentless affection had eventually worn him down, and he'd surrendered to the nightly presence at the end of the bed.

Setting his spade aside, Ivvár picked up the cat and crossed the garden until he stood beside Edda. "Sefa, Gorm." He smiled and inclined his head in greeting before placing Söl on the bench beside his wife.

"Ivvár," Sefa replied and looked relieved that his arrival had distracted her son from a further outburst.

"Edda, I fear it is unsafe for you or the babe to be out in this cold wind."

Edda's hand moved to cradle the swell of her stomach and shook her head, her lips forming a bemused smile.

"Women have endured much worse since the beginning of time, Ivvár. All will be well."

Sefa rose to her feet and adjusted her skirts. "Come, Gorm. We must be away now."

"Ivvár, you have chased them off!"

Sefa shook her head. "Nei. Truly, it is long past time we left. I will see that Gorm stretches the arm."

Edda rose to her feet and embraced Seda and Gorm, whispering a few words only for the boy's ears before pushing him toward his mother.

As Sefa walked toward the hall with one arm wrapped around her son, she paused and looked back over her shoulder. "Edda, you should listen to your husband. It is wise to rest when you are with child."

A wide grin split his face. Placing his hands on his hips, he rocked back on his heels. "Já. Hear that little wife? You should heed your husband."

A loud groan rang out through the garden.

Ivvár spun around to face the culprit.

Kal stood shaking his head at him. "Gods, Ivvár! Even I know not to tell a wife to heed her husband." Muttering at the foolishness of grown men, the boy returned to harvesting the last of the onions from the garden bed.

Arms wrapped around his waist and pulled him close. *Edda.* He looked down at her, his eyes devouring her soft, plump lips, the adorably upturned tilt of her nose, and those forest-green eyes staring at him from the shadows of her hood.

"Kal speaks wisely," she teased.

He pressed his lips to her forehead in a gentle kiss. "You know I merely wish to protect you and our son."

"Our first son." Quickly rising on her toes, Edda brushed her lips over his before settling back on her feet.

"More sons? You have seen it?"

Her eyes bright with joy, Edda smiled up at him and nodded. "The gods will bless us with many sons and a daughter. Now heed *me*, husband, and kiss me."

"As you wish, little wife." And he did, thoroughly.

AFTERWORD

Thank you so much for reading Edda and Ivvár's story. I hope you had a wonderful time with them. Authors love reviews. If you enjoyed this book, please consider leaving a review at your place of purchase.

To hear about new releases, you can sign up for my newsletter at **http://www.reethornton.com**

ALSO BY REE THORNTON

BELOVED VIKING

The shield-maiden must marry...

Heir to her father's Jarldom, Rúna Isaksson will soon ascend to replace him as leader, but first she must marry a warrior from another clan to form a powerful alliance. When her father creates a contest to determine the strongest suitor, Rúna demands to compete as well—if she wins, she can choose her own husband. However, she's shocked to discover that her first love is amongst the competitors, the man who abandoned her without looking back. She must not let him win.

A Viking warrior haunted by a dark past...

Jorvan Eriksson has returned from seeking his fortune to claim his childhood sweetheart, but the girl he left behind has become a battle-hardened shield-maiden with no intention of forgiving him. Jorvan has changed too—he now fights a darkness that lurks in his own mind. Somehow, he must conquer his demons to out-manoeuvre the other suitors and win the Viking games for Rúna's hand. Though victory alone will never be enough. He won't settle for anything less than reclaiming the future Jarl's heart.

FORBIDDEN VIKING

An Arabian Princess tastes freedom...

When Samara Abbasid's ship is attacked, she throws herself
overboard and seeks refuge in the Viking Jarldom of Gottland.
Claiming to be merely a scribe, she temporarily escapes her life of
duty and expectation, and is free to sample the Vikings ways. She
finds them as seductive as the strong Jarl, Valen. However, if Valen
discovers her royal status he could use her as leverage in his trade
negotiations with her father, the powerful Caliph. Worse, she must
soon return to the royal court and her upcoming arranged
marriage. But once she's tasted forbidden pleasure will she be able
to return to a life of duty...?

A Jarl bound by duty...

The most powerful Viking clans are assembling on the isle of
Gottland to celebrate Valen Eriksson's ascension to Jarl. So Valen is
furious to discover rogue Vikings have raided in his territory. Now
he must serve swift justice and protect the mysterious survivor
until he can return her the Abbasid Caliph. The last thing he needs
is to be tempted by the alluring scribe, not when he's sworn to
choose a bride from an allied Viking clan. His duty is clear, yet his
heart yearns...

WINTER VIKING

A Viking queen on the run...

Widow Ásta Helgesen's husband died years ago in a brutal attack that cost her everything she loved. For four years, she has lived as Ásta Oleander, hiding in plain sight as she mourns her husband. The one time she took a man to her furs, the crushing guilt overwhelmed her brief need to move and she vowed Dànel would be the last. Now the maniacal Jarl who killed her husband has discovered she's alive and is determined to make her his bride. He's dangerous, powerful and will stop at nothing to get what he wants. Forced to flee, Ásta journeys to the bitterly cold northlands to seek sanctuary in the isolated lands of a man she bedded once, and then rejected. Will he protect her from a murderer? Or has she made a terrible mistake?

A warrior with a painful past...

Following the death of his brother, Dànel Kvitfjell has returned to the Sami northlands to take over the shipping fleet that supports the family village. Yet everything reminds him of the tragedy that led to his childhood banishment and he realizes that, after more than a decade fostered with Vikings, his family now feel more like strangers. All he wants is to fulfill his duty to his people and return to life with his Viking comrades, but the unexpected arrival of Ásta and her dangerous secrets jeopardizes everything. Why has the woman who rejected his affections sought him out? Forced to flee deep into the wilderness with Ásta, Dànel must confront the painful past that haunts him. Can he protect Ásta from both the man hunting her *and* the harsh winter land where one mistake can steal those you love?

VIKING BETRAYED

A wife with a dark past...

Two years ago, thief Helga Tannrsson made the fatal mistake of falling for her mark. To marry the man her heart desired, she faked her own death and adopted the noblewoman persona that had been her cover story when she'd met Ulf. Now Helga should be happy— she has the life of her dreams, yet she's caught in a trap of her own making. Living a lie is harder than she'd imagined, her deep-seated mistrust of men still haunts her, and she's unable to even bare her body to her husband when they make love. As Helga struggles to hold onto the fraying threads of her marriage, a shadow from her past reappears.

The Viking who loves her...

For much of his life, overseer of the city's defences Ulf Eriksson felt unworthy of his prestigious family name. Claiming a Viking noblewoman as his bride had finally allowed him to hold his head high as an Eriksson brother. Yet all is not well within his marriage. He'd hoped that his beloved Helga would come to trust him, but she remains frustratingly closed-off and distant, not even disrobing for the marriage bed. When outlaws breach the city wall and are revealed to be Helga's kin, the shocking truth about his wife is laid bare. Devastated, shamed, and with his reputation in tatters, Ulf doubts whether his marriage was even real or just one long con. Had the thief that stole his heart ever loved him? And, after all the lies and betrayal can he trust her again?

Milton Keynes UK
Ingram Content Group UK Ltd.
UKHW010716180823
427095UK00001B/65